AWARDS

Shortlisted for 2012 Eric Hoffer New Horizon Award for debut authors.
Honorable Mention for 2012 Eric Hoffer Commercial Fiction Award

REVIEWS

"Extremely interesting and cleverly written-I was completely enthralled! Lucy Bertoldi, *Historical Novel Society*.

"A gripping, well-researched historical novel, revealing a violent age. Cecylee and the other characters are well-drawn, with great subtlety and depth." Lindsay Townsend, author of *To Touch the Knight*.

"The author immerses the reader in a complex and vivid world that is depicted with persuasive confidence." Curtis Sittenfeld, author of *American Wife*.

"A wonderful novel to introduce Cecily Neville and historical biographical fiction to young female readers." Mirella Patzer, author of *The Pendant*.

"Haggard delivers a swift epic that is both entertaining and informing. The writing is crisp and clear, the characters well-defined, and the emotion overflowing. This book has something for everyone—romance, intrigue, and plenty of action." *US Review of Books*, May 2012.

TWO MURDERS REAPED

The fourth in a saga about the Yorks, Lancasters and Nevilles,

whose family feud started the Wars of the Roses.

Told by Cecily "Cecylee" Neville (1415-1495),

the Thwarted Queen

Cynthia Sally Haggard

Spun Stories Press
Washington DC 20036

This book is a work of fiction. Names, characters, places, and incidents either are products of the author's imagination or are used fictitiously. Any resemblance to actual events or locales or persons, living or dead, is entirely coincidental.

Published by Spun Stories Press

Designed by Cynthia Sally Haggard

Manufactured in the United States of America

ISBN: 0984816933
ISBN-13: 978-0-9848169-3-4

LCCN: TX 7-473-955

For my dear friend Beth Gessert Franks
for all her endurance of Cecylee

Contents

Acknowledgments

This book took me seven years to write. I could not have done it without the help of many people. The first person who deserves thanks is my friend Beth Franks, a talented writer in her own right, who patiently went through several drafts of *Thwarted Queen*, and made innumerable suggestions for improvement.

Next, I want to thank my wonderful editor Catherine Adams, formerly of the *Iowa Book Doctors* now of *Inkslinger Editing*, for her structural editing of the manuscript early on, and the many helpful suggestions she made then that brought the novel to a new level. This summer, Catherine did a magnificent job in the line-by-line content and copyediting, gently pruning the manuscript to give it what I hope is a polished, professional feel. Any mistakes are my own!

I also wish to thank Lord Barnard of Raby Castle in County Durham for his interest in my novel, and for allowing Clifton Sutcliffe, the docent, to take me on a personal tour of Cecily's childhood home in July 2007. Mr. Sutcliffe showed me the Keep where Cecylee was locked up by her father, and explained to me about the wooden walkways that criss-crossed Castle Raby to make passage from one tower to another easy in the event of a raid. I am also indebted to him for bringing to my attention John Wolstenholme Cobb's *History and Antiquities of Berkhamsted*, in which he quotes *The Orders and Rules of the Princess Cecill.*

I wish to thank the United States Military Academy Department of History for allowing me to use the map of England and France circa 1422, and for Emerson Kent in helping me to find it.

I was privileged to take classes with many wonderful teachers during my long journey with *TQ*. I wish to thank Mark Spencer, professor of English and Dean of the School of Arts and Humanities at the University of Arkansas at Monticello for his class *Successful Self-Publishing*, given during the spring of 2011; Curtis Sittenfeld, author of *American*

Wife, for her sensitive reading of the novel during the *2010 Napa Valley Writer's Workshop*; Amy Rennert of the Amy Rennert Agency for her class *Secrets of Publishing Success* given at Book Passage in Corte Madera CA, during the fall of 2006; Janis Cooke-Newman, author of *Mary: Mrs. A. Lincoln*, for her invaluable help on the end of the novel; Michael Neff, creator of *Web del Sol*, for his wonderful classes on craft at the *2005 Harper's Ferry Workshop*; Junse Kim, who taught *Introduction to Fiction: You Can't Build a House without Foundations* and Otis Haschemeyer, who taught *Introduction to the Novel* at the *Writing Salon* in Bernal Heights San Francisco during the fall of 2004. I could not have written and published my novel without the help of these professionals.

My friend Beth Robertson deserves thanks for sharing her expertise on Chaucer, and her knowledge of subversive activity amongst medieval ladies, who would often read material that would not have pleased their husbands. Such inflammatory scrolls were secreted in the saddle bags of Abbesses and other ladies, who were ostensibly just making a social call.

I wish to thank the following writers for reading the manuscript and making useful suggestions: Kristin Abkemeyer, Myrna Loy Ashby, Sharyn Bowman, Peter Brown, Julie Corwin, Eric Goldman, Joy Jones, Phil Kurata, Nadine Leavitt-Siak, Michelle McGurk, Amanda Miller, Rose Murphy, Nicole Nelson, Dan Newman, Desirée Parker, Walter Simson, Kevin Singer, Judy Wertheimer, Jun Yan.

Last but not least, I wish to thank the talented Heather Hayes for donating her time to model for Cecylee; her friend, Whitney Arostegui, for donating her time to shoot the photos that were used for the cover of the novel; Dave Graham for donating his time to convert my cover images to CMYK mode and teaching me to make the necessary edits; my husband Georges Rey for prodding me to continue with Cecylee, and my sister Melanie, for giving me the idea in the first place.

Plantagenet

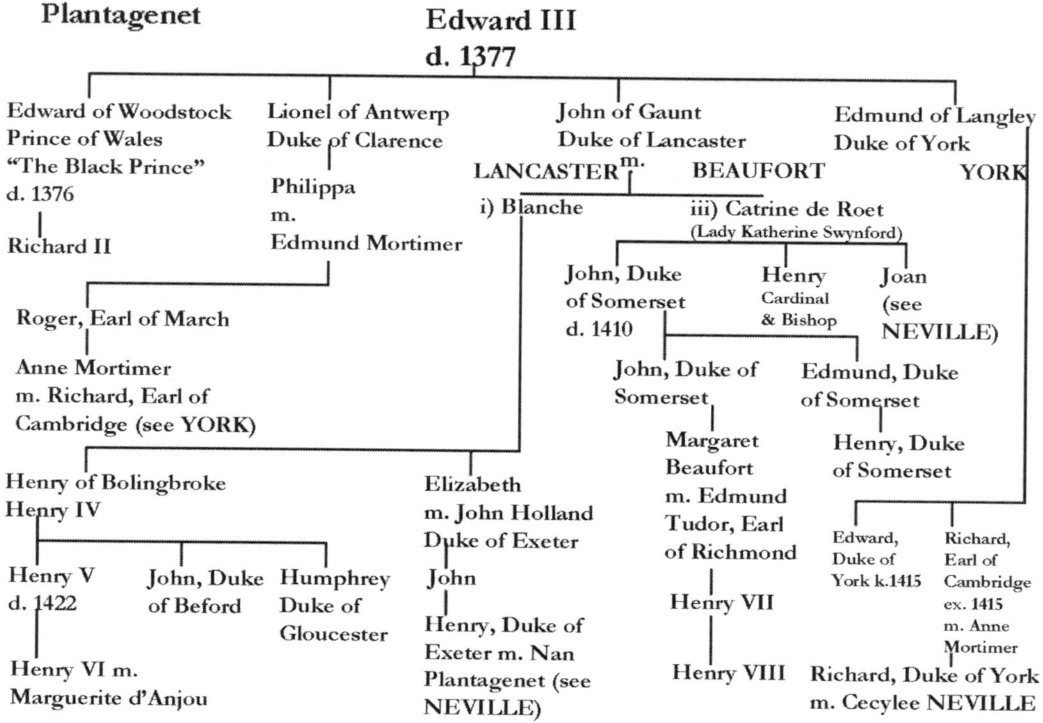

Neville

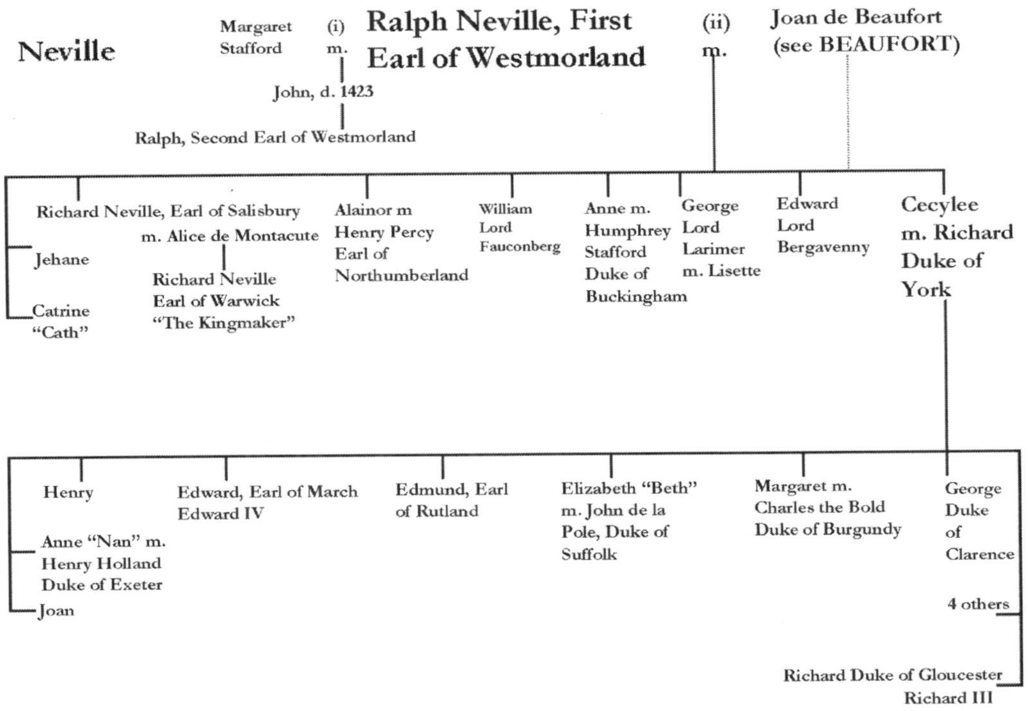
Margaret Stafford
(i) m.
Ralph Neville, First Earl of Westmorland
(ii) m.
Joan de Beaufort (see BEAUFORT)
John, d. 1423
Ralph, Second Earl of Westmorland
Richard Neville, Earl of Salisbury m. Alice de Montacute
Richard Neville Earl of Warwick "The Kingmaker"
Jehane
Catrine "Cath"
Alainor m Henry Percy Earl of Northumberland
William Lord Fauconberg
Anne m. Humphrey Stafford Duke of Buckingham
George Lord Larimer m. Lisette
Edward Lord Bergavenny
Cecylee m. Richard Duke of York
Henry
Anne "Nan" m. Henry Holland Duke of Exeter
Joan
Edward, Earl of March Edward IV
Edmund, Earl of Rutland
Elizabeth "Beth" m. John de la Pole, Duke of Suffolk
Margaret m. Charles the Bold Duke of Burgundy
George Duke of Clarence
4 others
Richard Duke of Gloucester Richard III

ENGLAND & FRANCE

After the second English invasion 1422.

Green represents both England & English France.

Orange represents territory loyal to the Dauphin Charles of France.

BOOK IV

To all sicke men is given a lybertye to have all such thinges as may be to their ease...
If any man fall impotente,
he hath styll the same wages that he had when he might doe his best service,
during my ladyes lyfe.

FROM ORDERS AND RULES OF THE PRINCESS CECILL
QUOTED BY JOHN WOLSTENHOLME COBB (1883)
HISTORY & ANTIQUITIES OF BERKHAMSTED

Chapter 1
Ludlow, Welsh Marches
October 13, 1459

A low, rumbling sound could be heard faintly in the distance. It grew louder. It shimmered with the addition of the high jingling sounds of harness and bridle. A trumpet sounded a blast, and the folk of Ludlow came to their doors, braced for the worst. A chill wind lifted my veil, fluttering from the point of my tall henin. To greet the queen, I arrayed myself in a dress of pale green damask woven with gold thread, worn over a violet chemise. I had not thought to put on my mantle, believing we would be back in the castle soon. But the neckline of my gown was edged in miniver, and that helped to ward off the cold.

My three children stood with me; Margaret, running a rosary through her fingers as she recited the prayers I'd taught her; George, shifting impatiently from one foot to the other as he fingered the exquisitely bejeweled dagger his father had given him; and Richard, who had turned seven only ten days before. Richard was dressed in his favorite shade of grey, which set off his grey-blue eyes. In contrast to his brother, he was quiet; far too quiet. The only emotion he showed was when he clutched at my hand when, with a roar, the queen's army flooded into the marketplace of Ludlow. The sound was deafening, as the children and I were suddenly surrounded by the grinning, leering faces of unwashed, unshaven men, brandishing weapons.

"Well, well, and what have we here?" said one of these churls, sidling up to Margaret, eyeing her in a thoroughly disgusting fashion.

Margaret had dressed in her best sky-blue damask, setting off her creamy skin and rich dark-brown hair. She edged closer to me, shivering. How I wished that I'd made her put on her thick fur mantle, for she needed it now, more for protection from leering eyes than for warmth.

I stepped forward. "I am Cecylee, Duchess of York. I wish to speak to the Duke of Somerset." Henry Beaufort, now Duke of Somerset, had been given command of the Lancastrian army at the age of three-and-twenty years. I knew little of this young man, but surely he could not be as bad as his father, who'd been one of Richard's greatest enemies.

"You do, do you?" answered the fellow. "I'm sure he'd like to speak to you too." This remark was followed by loud guffaws from the other men.

A film of sweat blossomed on my forehead, dampening my wimple. I flushed and clasped my hands together to still their shaking. I hadn't thought that the men might refuse my request.

But a stir started quickly, and the Duke of Somerset rode into view, followed by Humphrey Stafford, Duke of Buckingham, and Henry Percy, Earl of Northumberland, the commanders of the queen's army. With one motion of Somerset's hand, the churls fell back. He dismounted.

"Duchess," he called as I curtseyed low. "Where is your lord? Your brother? Your older sons?"

"They are not here," I replied.

I put my hands on my boys' shoulders to remind them of their manners. They bowed under the gentle pressure of my fingers.

"I am here as you see, with my younger children. I beg you to be merciful."

"Beg?" His eyebrows shot up. He put his hand to his chin, considering. "I don't think I have ever seen you beg, Duchess Cecylee."

My cheeks warmed. I had not expected to be forced to answer the accusation of Proud Cis now. I looked at the ground. It was filthy. If I knelt down, I would ruin the gown Jenet had finished only the other day.

I bit my lip, shot Somerset a look. He stood there, hand to chin, one eyebrow raised, regarding me with ill-concealed amusement. In the distance, the folk of Ludlow edged away from their doorways, forming a large silent crowd. They craned their necks, and I recognized the pleasant young woman I employed to clean my chamber. What about those poor people? One ruined dress was nothing. They were my people, I was their liege lady. It was my duty to protect them.

Without a second thought, I knelt in the filth. It squelched noisily as I lowered myself to my knees, and an unpleasant smell assailed my nostrils. I looked up and raised both hands in supplication.

"My lord of Somerset, I beg you. Be merciful to the good folk of Ludlow. They have done nothing wrong."

"Where is York?" snapped Northumberland, coming up by Somerset's side.

Somerset regarded Northumberland, then turned back to me. "We are prepared to be merciful to you and yours," he said, "if you tell us the whereabouts of York, March, Rutland, Salisbury, and Warwick."

I froze.

"You're upsetting Mama," put in George, suddenly. He stepped forward, his hand on his dagger.

George had turned ten yesterday, and it had taken hours to get him ready, for he was fond of clothes. He had already discarded twelve suits before settling on a bright green tunic decorated with gold thread.

"It matches your gown, Mama," he said, smiling his charming smile, so that I wouldn't be angry with him for being made to wait.

Before I could prevent him, George continued, "You shouldn't make Mama kneel in this filth. She has ruined her best gown."

My sides ached as I held in my breath. The last thing I wanted was for my boy to speak out.

Fortunately, Somerset laughed. "And who are you, my little lordling?"

I put my hand on George's arm and gently withdrew his hand from his dagger. "This is my son George."

Somerset pointedly turned his back on the boy and leaned in closer. "Out with it, my lady. I think you know where the Yorkist lords are."

I lowered my lashes and stared at the ground. What could I say? I knew that once these Lancastrian lords got their hands on them, they'd never come back alive.

"Torch their houses!" someone bellowed.

I scrambled to my feet and tugged at Somerset's sleeve. "My lord, I beg you. Be merciful. What have these people done?"

He disengaged my arm roughly, and spat out a response. "You can stop all this, my fine lady." He eyed my spattered skirts. "Just tell us where they are."

"Never!" I cried.

A high neighing made me turn. Marguerite d'Anjou, Queen of England, dressed in cloth of gold, sat on a black horse. As the queen eyed me grimly, I journeyed back in time to when I'd last seen her and asked for a pension of one thousand marks in return for Richard's loyalty. My cheeks warmed, ice crawled up my spine. What was I doing here with three children? I shouldn't be putting their lives in danger. I should have gone to the priory at Wigmore as Edward had suggested. After all, the queen could kidnap the boys. Why wouldn't she? She had already taken two of Salisbury's sons.

The queen's hard voice cut through my wandering thoughts. "My lady York, well met. I see you have mislaid your husband."

George opened his mouth, and I put a hand on his shoulder to forestall him. Perhaps I could persuade her to be reasonable, one woman to another. Wrinkling my nose, I again lowered myself to my knees as the men guffawed, making cracks about the state of my garments.

"Madam," I said, "I beg you for the love of Christ, be merciful to the folk of Ludlow. Prevent your soldiers from torching their homes, from looting, from rampaging."

I paused, and bit my lip.

"You lied!" exclaimed the Queen, pointing her whip at me. "You came to me all those years ago, begging me not to notice your lord's treachery. Why should I listen to anything you say now? You are two-faced madame. You are duplicitous."

I trembled as I bowed my head. I learned then that Marguerite never forgot the wrongs done to her.

"So you imagine we are animals," continued Marguerite. She raised her hand. "Let us show my lady York."

She let her hand fall, and the Lancastrian beasts set to work. By the time they'd finished, Ludlow was nothing more than an ash-heap. When they'd finished with the town, they went into the castle, and all of our costly furnishings, clothing, and books were thrown about, looted, and burned.

I was forced to watch with my three children. The worst part of this harrowing and humiliating experience was the sound. The sound of horses panicking, people screaming, fire roaring, people begging for their lives, women pleading to be spared from rape.

By the time they'd finished, dusk was falling. It was the worst day of my life. Most of all, my children had to go through it. Margaret wept silently, her face smudged from the smoke blackening everything. George clutched his dagger so hard it made his fingers bleed. But the worst was the effect it had on seven-year-old Richard. He disappeared. I could not rouse him. He just stared at me. Silent.

At length, they arrested and escorted us to Stafford Castle, the residence of the Duke of Buckingham and my sister Anne. I hadn't seen much of Anne since we were children, and I wondered how she would be now. After all, her husband and mine were mortal enemies.

"Cecylee."

I turned, and there she was. My sister, only looking older.

She came forward, lines of concern etched on her face, and kissed me on the cheek.

I don't know why it was, perhaps because she suddenly reminded me of Mama. But suddenly, I broke down.

Anne took in the sight of my three children, filthy and exhausted, and immediately ordered hot baths and refreshments. She took me by the hand and led me into her chamber, where I was given a much-needed bath and some fresh garments. Anne's servants arrived, bearing hot possets, and we sent the children to bed.

"Where is your husband?" she whispered as we sat by the fire.

"You know I cannot tell you that."

She sighed. "Wherever he may be, he has left you to bear all this by yourself. Why, leaving a lady and three children to face down a whole army—"

"That was my idea," I interrupted, my cheeks burning. "My lord was against it, but he had no choice."

"You mean he was not able to anticipate the situation?"

"No," I replied, looking away. "Things moved so fast."

"I worry greatly for your safety, Cecylee," said Anne, leaning forward and patting my hand. "If a lord cannot protect his wife and children, who will?"

I hung my head as I knotted my fingers together. My feelings simmered just out of reach.

Chapter 2
Stafford Castle, Staffordshire
Autumn 1459 to Summer 1460

Richard and his allies determined to launch one final, decisive attack against the Court Party, and this naturally meant invading England from Ireland and Calais.

I knew little of these matters, for I was under house arrest and scarcely any news got through. Anne was kind, but loyal to her husband, the Duke of Buckingham, and she never discussed matters of political import. For the first time since that fateful summer when I'd met Blaybourne, I was separated from Richard. I couldn't even send or receive letters.

As the months passed with no word, my feelings gradually unraveled. I was furious with him for blundering yet again, leaving the children and me in such a perilous situation. I'd never seen an army before and had no idea the situation could be so dire. I imagined that I would kneel before the Lancastrian commanders and they would honor my requests. They would lead me back to Ludlow Castle and then march on somewhere else. It never occurred to me that they might sack and burn the village of Ludlow, loot and destroy my possessions, and force me to watch the horror of it all with three children. Of course, Richard must have known how bad things could've been. But he'd fled anyway.

As I saw the damage that had been done to the children, I grew angrier and angrier. Margaret seemed unable to stop weeping. George talked about killing people with a disquieting light in his eyes. But Richard was the child who worried me the most, for he did not seem like a normal seven-year-old. During the day, he was silent. At night, he couldn't sleep from the nightmares that haunted him.

I tried to make life as normal as I could for the children. I had Richard sleep with me at night, while George and Margaret slept together. But what was I to do about Margaret's constant weeping? It grated on everyone's nerves.

One day, we sat with the ladies of Anne's household, embroidering, when I noticed how accomplished Margaret had become.

"My sweet," I said, as an idea struck me. "How would you like to embroider some shirts for your father?"

"Father?" whispered Margaret, after looking around to be sure no one was listening.

I smiled sadly. Margaret was already acting far older than her thirteen years.

"It would mean a great deal to him."

Margaret smiled for the first time in many weeks.

I kissed her, then my thoughts turned to the other Richard, my youngest son.

"It worries me that Richard is so silent," I murmured as Margaret dried her tears, opened her needlework box, and started hunting for skeins of silk. "Does he talk at all when I'm not around?"

"Not really," replied Margaret, threading her needle. "He seems to enjoy reading books."

Wasn't that an unusual occupation for a seven-year-old? "I would like you to spend more time with him. He needs to be with people."

"I could ask him to walk with me when I go outside with the others." Anne had four daughters living at home who were around the same age as my children.

"A good thought, my love," I said rising, and smiling at her. "And now, I must see to George."

With his father gone, George saw himself as the head of the family and strutted about self-importantly, earning him laughs and sneers from those of Buckingham's affinity. I sighed as I made my way to his chamber. The boy was charming and intelligent, but—

"My lady," called Jenet softly. She came forward, and put her mouth close to my ear. "The London merchants have given my lord of Warwick eighteen thousand pounds."

I stared at her. That was an enormous sum of money. It could only mean that the merchants were full weary of the bad government of the king and had actually paid Warwick to invade England. I opened my mouth when Jenet indicated with her eyes that someone was watching.

I turned slowly around. It was Anne.

"Cecylee!" she exclaimed, kissing my cheek. "What are you doing here?"

"Looking for George," I replied. "I am worried about him. He has so much energy and not enough to do."

"That's very true," said Anne, laughing, taking my arm.

Had she noticed Jenet? I guided Anne downstairs in the opposite direction. "George isn't a scholar," I continued. "He needs something to channel his considerable energies." *And dull those bloodthirsty thoughts.*

"'Tis time he became a page," remarked Anne. "Perhaps he could serve his uncle Buckingham."

I thanked her as I smiled my misgivings away. I hoped George would behave himself, not speak out of turn, nor divulge matters best to be silent about. Most of all I hoped that George's position in Buckingham's household did not mean that he was being held hostage against the good behavior of his lord father.

❦

In June of 1460, my nephew Warwick arrived in Kent. My lady queen was unable to prevent this from happening—or prevent the arrival of my brother Salisbury, or that of my son Edward, Earl of March. Her sailors mutinied, and thus the Yorkist ships passed them by, unmolested.

I bit my nails to the quick on hearing this news, whispered to me by Jenet. Warwick was taking a great risk by occupying a town in Kent, for his lands and sphere of influence lay in the distant north and west. This meant that he had to take London before he could reach his lands.

He was held in such esteem and affection by the people of Kent and the Londoners, however, I need not have worried. When he sent messages asking for support, the mayors of the little Kentish towns readily complied. Soon, men flocked to Warwick's standard in large numbers. Then, though my lady queen tried to prevent the Yorkist lords from entering the city of Canterbury, their sympathizers gave them the keys. The gates were flung open and the people gave Warwick, Salisbury, and March a warm welcome. During their short stay, Warwick secured the good offices of the papal legate, which had the effect of encouraging the bishops to join the Yorkist cause.

News of the invasion had by now reached London. The mayor of that city, anxious that he not been seen as treasonous sent a cautiously worded message to Warwick, advising him that he would not be permitted to enter.

It did not matter.

Warwick had so many friends among the merchants and the people that the mayor was persuaded to reconsider. On the second day of July, the gates of London were thrown open, and the Yorkists lords entered the city followed by around forty thousand armed men.

"Their plan now must be to gain control over the king," I murmured to Jenet as we sat outside with our sewing. Stafford Castle was quiet, all the menfolk gone to the queen's army, commanded by Buckingham.

"Your son Edward and my lord of Warwick are to leave London for Coventry where the king resides," she whispered.

However, the king left Coventry and marched to Northampton to take refuge in the almost impenetrable Fen country surrounding the Isle of Ely. The queen's army arrived in Northampton to protect the king, drawing itself up in battle order.

On the tenth of July, Warwick's army arrived. He tried to avoid battle by sending the papal legate and other bishops to the king to beg an airing of the grievances of the Yorkist lords. My lord of Buckingham accused the bishops of hypocrisy and advised the king to pay them no heed.

At two o'clock in the afternoon, with the rain teeming down, watched by the papal legate and the Archbishop of Canterbury, Warwick ordered his trumpeters to sound the call to battle. Edward commanded the vanguard. His advance across the Nene marshes was met with a deadly series of volleys from the Lancastrian archers.

Chapter 3
Stafford Castle, Staffordshire
July 1460

As I stepped onto the castle battlements, a cooling breeze lifted my veil. I looked for George but he was nowhere to be seen. Thank goodness that George had been considered too young to fight; for Buckingham would certainly have taken him when he left the castle a fortnight ago. I could only marvel at my good fortune. Buckingham had been courteous, and more importantly, had refrained from making hostages out of my two boys. I thanked God every day for their safe deliverance while I awaited tidings of the latest conflict.

Though it was hot, the commander of the garrison at Stafford Castle did not allow his men to relax. All were stationed at their posts and had to remain there, while Anne directed her servants to pour watered-down ale. Leaving Anne behind me, I wandered along the parapet encircling the castle wall. I came upon George engaged in assisting a squire with the commander's heavy armor. While the two boys tightened buckles and tied laces, the commander scanned the horizon.

I watched for a moment. This son reminded me most forcibly of my father. Like him, George was an amusing and lively companion. Even his gestures were similar as he told jokes. His bright eyes took everything in, and I sighed once more with sorrow as I thought of the horrors he'd seen that day at Ludlow. At that moment, he glanced up.

"Mama!" he called, looking like the young lad he was.

I smiled into his blue-green eyes. "Well met, my son."

"And how does my nephew?" remarked Anne, coming up silently behind me.

"Well, madam," responded George gravely. "I've been learning all about how to clean armor, and which order the pieces go on."

"Lord George has a quick wit," remarked the commander, bowing. "He'll make a fine squire some day."

There was an awkward pause. How I wished this war would end. I turned to look at the horizon, which shimmered in the heat.

"Someone's coming," remarked George in a whisper.

I shot my son a look, then scanned the horizon again.

"To your posts!" roared the commander. "Ladies, I must ask you to wait below."

"George!" I exclaimed as fear gripped me.

"Mama!" he exclaimed, mimicking my tone.

I watched helpless as George scampered away.

"Leave him be," said Anne quietly. "He'll only fret if he's mewed up with us."

I sighed as I follow Anne downstairs. I went to my bedchamber to see Richard, who was feeling poorly. I wondered if he would survive this latest bout of illness. I'd lost so many children, two daughters and four sons who'd never grown up, locked in my memory as the small children they'd been when taken up to heaven. I recited the litany now as I looked down at Richard's wan face: *Joan, Henry, William, John, Thomas, Ursula.*

Sitting down, I took Richard's small hand in mine. What kind of man would he be? He was tenacious. He'd shown that by the way he clung on through the worst of his illnesses. He was already showing the promise of a fine mind, preferring to play chess and read books. And he was preternaturally serious, just like his father.

I smiled, thinking of Richard. We'd met in December 1423 at Castle Raby. I'd been a lively eight-year-old sent out one bright December day to tend to my roses when I saw a strange boy watching me.

When asked who he was, he drew himself up stiffly. "Richard, Duke of York."

I tossed him some pert reply and turned my back on him while humming a favorite air. When I turned around, he was still there. "You're so serious!" I exclaimed. "Don't you ever smile?"

At that, he had smiled. Tentatively.

And now, I hadn't seen him in nine months. I'd grown accustomed to life without Richard, and found that it suited me. Most of all, I reveled in the freedom of making my own decisions without the need to consult him. I felt a twinge of guilt. How was he faring in Ireland? I'd heard nothing—

A door banged, and then there was the sound of heavy feet. I bent over my son to hide my fear. The child was stirring.

"Mama?" he said sleepily. Then suddenly his pale face lit with a smile.

I swung around.

"Edward!" I exclaimed.

Any misgivings I had about Edward vanished as I took him in, standing in front of me, tall and gleaming in his suit of armor. I thought he'd never looked so handsome, and my heart caught in my throat.

"Mother," he said, bowing. Then he kissed me on the cheek before turning to the bed. "And how goes brother Richard?"

To my amazement, Richard pushed himself up in bed and leaned forward eagerly. Under his older brother's smile, Richard shed years, looking like a little boy rather than an old man.

"I bought you a gift," remarked Edward.

How had Edward found the time to get his little brother a gift?

Edward reached into the folds of his tunic and drew out a horseshoe. "'Tis from White York, my stallion that helped me win the battle."

"Battle? What battle?" I asked.

"All in good time, Mother," replied Edward. He turned to Richard. "Tuck it under your pillow for good luck."

"I wish I could fight like you," remarked Richard, gazing at Edward with shining eyes.

"You do fight," said Edward, patting his shoulder. At that moment, the door blew open, and George entered, followed by Margaret. "Tell us the news!"

Edward gave an account of the Battle of Northampton, and I could hardly believe he was alive. "You were under fire from the Lancastrian archers, and the weather was atrocious?"

"Aye," agreed Edward. "The mud was thick and viscous. That's how White York lost his shoe. But the Lancastrians could not fire their cannon because the rain was teeming down. When we reached their defenses, Lord Grey de Ruthun gave the signal, and his men helped us over the barricades."

I clasped a hand over my mouth. Edmund Grey, a faithful supporter of the Lancastrian cause, threw his allegiance in with the House of York? "He should be rewarded," I breathed, drying my hands on my handkerchief. "I'm most grateful that Lady Fortune was with you that day."

Suddenly, my mind jolted awake. What was Edward doing at Stafford Castle?

I turned to him. "Buckingham?"

Edward looked grim. "I bear bad tidings. He's dead."

Chapter 4
July to October 1460

The Battle of Northampton lasted the space of one half of an hour, and at the end of it, Warwick, March, and Salisbury took possession of the king and conducted him to Delapré Abbey. My lady queen fled with her son to Scotland.

Though I was free from house arrest, my heart bled as I said my farewells to my sister Anne. But she seemed to take the news of Buckingham's passing with a kind of stoic resignation. Her family flocked to her side. Their silences and stares convinced me to be quick in my leave.

Now I was free. As free as a lark to soar up into the air and sing merrily. I traveled to Baynard's Castle, my London residence, taking the children with me.

On the eight day of September, Richard, together with Edmund, returned from Ireland. He sent a message asking me to meet with him in Hereford. I sighed, for it was not going to be easy to be Richard's wife again after the freedom of the past few months.

Leaving the children behind in London, I took a horse litter, choosing this somewhat queenly mode of transportation because I did not feel like riding the hundred or so miles. Taking a litter hung with blue velvet curtains and drawn between two pairs of fine horses was not only a stylish way of greeting my long-absent husband. It also had the effect of prolonging my journey.

While I journeyed, I had the leisure to ponder. How unfortunate that Richard was not a person to whom folk warmed easily, for he had many good qualities. He cared deeply about the people and had been loyal to King Henry until the King's misrule had driven him to take up arms. But Richard also had his flaws. He was arrogant, he was proud, and as always, he was too serious for his own good. While I journeyed to Hereford, I wondered how he would be now.

When finally I saw him, it was as if a stranger were standing there. Richard had grown stout during his sojourn in

Ireland. His hair and beard had gone grey, and there were harsh lines around his mouth. But when he caught sight of me, his smile made him look like the young man who'd courted me.

He eagerly helped me down from the litter, so caught up in greeting me that he didn't notice the expensive mode of transportation. "Cis! You look as fair as ever. Christ! How I've missed you."

I smiled as I submitted to his embraces. Then I looked around. "Why are your men in such livery? They are bearing the Royal Arms." I turned to stare at him. "That's treasonous, Richard."

Richard's mouth set in a grim line, following the creases of the new lines around his mouth. "I wish to make my pretensions to the throne clear. I will not be gainsaid by anyone, not even you, Cis."

And with that, he strode off.

❦

Richard was not in the most communicative of moods as he and I traveled to London at the head of a large retinue. I tried to persuade him to discuss his plans with me. To no avail. Had Richard even consulted with his allies? The night before our arrival in London, growing anxious, I forced the issue.

I ordered the cook to prepare Richard's favorite dishes. I had my women dress me in a gown of lilac brocade, for it was one of Richard's favorite colors. Then I sent a message inviting him to my tent.

By the time he arrived, I'd given instructions to put thick carpets on the floors, light candles, and arrange flowers. A group of musicians sat in one corner, playing some of his favorite airs. He smiled as I took him by the hand and bade him sit beside me.

First I presented him with gifts from the children, including Margaret's beautifully embroidered shirts. Then I signaled for the servants to bring out the meal. Only when he'd finished eating and was well watered with wine did I broach the topic. Signaling for the servants to leave, I stroked his hand.

"My lord," I began in a low tone, leaning forward, "What mean you to do once we arrive in London?"

"I mean to claim the throne for myself."

"That is your right, but do others know of your plans?"

Richard's eyes went from being the gentle grey-blue of waves rippling by the shoreline to the flinty grey of a winter sky. "Why should I tell anyone? Think you I should ask permission?"

I stroked his hand again, for he was so irritable these days. "Of course not," I said soothingly. "But don't you think it might be better to make sure they agree with you?"

"Of course they agree with me. That's why we're fighting, isn't it?"

I sighed and pressed ahead. Richard could be heavy weather, but it was imperative to nudge him in the right direction. If he were going to succeed in his ambitions, he had to get the backing of the magnates, as well as the citizens of London. "Does Salisbury know that you're marching to London to take the throne of England?"

The silence stretched on. "No," said Richard reluctantly, crumbling his bread.

"I think," I whispered, "I think you should dictate a letter to him, and to the other magnates, explaining what you intend to do."

Richard frowned and stopped crumbling bread. Finally he nodded. "I give you my word."

I sagged with relief and gave him my most dazzling smile.

On the tenth day of October, Richard and I arrived in London. Much to the marvel of the folk of the City of London, our trumpeters bore the sovereign arms of England. We proceeded to Westminster Hall where Parliament was to meet. Dismounting at the door, Richard caused the sword of state to be borne before him. He strode through the throng of magnates and made his way to the throne, whereon he placed his hand. Placing his hand on the throne was the clearest signal Richard could give that he thought he should be king.

There was dead silence.

I looked for my relatives, for Salisbury and Warwick, confident that they knew and approved of this gesture. I expected them to come forward and acclaim Richard as their sovereign.

The silence continued, dismay on even friendly faces.

They were completely ignorant of his plans.

Mortified, I would have vanished in a puff of smoke at that instant if I could. Richard had lied to me. I looked at his shadowed face as he stared at the throne. He'd never done that before. What did it mean?

Richard lifted his head and flushed purple. "I am the heir general of King Richard II, and I tell you, I have waited too long. I shall be crowned King Richard III on All Hallows Day."

There was silence. All Hallows Day was less than three weeks away.

Archbishop Bourchier of Canterbury, the kinsman by marriage Richard had placed in that position so many years ago, came forward: "My lord. Perhaps you should obtain an audience with King Henry to discuss your claim."

Richard bristled. "I should obtain an audience with Henry of Lancaster?" he spat. "Say, rather, he should seek an audience with me. He is the usurper, descended from a line of usurpers, who illegally wrested the throne from King Richard II." Richard's voice grew louder and louder during this speech until he was bellowing at the magnates in that echoing hall.

He swept them one final look of disgust, then stormed out.

Conversation buzzed as soon as he disappeared. With flaming cheeks, I took the opportunity to slip away to Baynard's Castle. I ordered the main meal to be served and pushed my food around my plate while waiting for Richard to return. Had the many years of frustration not only soured his temper but also turned him into a liar? Eventually, Richard stormed in again, surrounded by men-at-arms. Without greeting me, he went to the sideboard to pour himself some wine.

Suddenly Warwick appeared. "Why didn't you consult us?" he roared, too angry to bother with a greeting. "This is madness. Why should our lord king be deposed now? He's ruled us for thirty-eight years. There's no precedent for your arrogance."

"How can you stand by a king who has promulgated decades of misrule upon this land?" Richard shot back.

Warwick came closer. "We took oaths of allegiance. Including you. He is our anointed king before God. Surely you're not thinking of arrogating the power of God to yourself."

Richard clenched his fingers around his wine-cup. "Kings have been deposed before. Henry's grandfather usurped the throne from King Richard II."

"Does your cursed ambition know no bounds?" bellowed Warwick. "King Richard was a tyrant, King Henry is a good man. He's saintly and pious. He's been good to the magnates, and you took an oath of allegiance to him."

This noisy row drew the whole household. Seventeen-year-old Rutland now appeared. When he saw Warwick castigating his father, he approached his cousin. "Fair sir, be not angry, for you know that we have the true right to the crown and that my lord and father here must have it."

Warwick flushed and bit his lip. For Rutland was correct. Richard had the better claim to the throne.

Eighteen-year-old Edward had been lounging at the table cracking nuts, seemingly uninterested in the row. But now he looked up and remarked, "Brother, 'tis not wise to vex Warwick."

Warwick smiled. Turning away from Richard and Rutland, he made a great show of speaking only to Edward.

Chapter 5
Palace of Westminster, London
October 16, 1460

Norfolk, premier duke and earl of the realm, eyed Richard grimly. "We have taken our oaths, and we stand by that."

Richard signaled to his scribe, who unrolled the parchment and set it on the table. "This shows that I am the rightful claimant to the throne," he said loudly. "This is my genealogy, showing my descent from King Edward III. I am descended from his second son, Lionel of Antwerp, through my mother, Lady Anne de Mortimer. My cousin Henry of Lancaster is descended from his third son, John of Gaunt."

Richard no longer referred to Henry VI as king, he was always *Henry of Lancaster*. I looked at Richard, trying to follow his mood. We stood in the great hall of Westminster Palace as Richard formally presented his claim to the great magnates of the land. At least he was calmer than he'd been a week ago. This time, he'd asked Salisbury and Warwick for their opinion. They advised him to go to the lords without them, to see more clearly what kind of support he would get.

What would Richard be like as king? I didn't like to think about it. He had many enemies and lacked the ability to deal with them. His temper was short and being an unpopular king would shorten it further. He was stubborn and too arrogant to take advice. I'd seen these traits grow worse as he gained power; worst of all, his actions might harm the children. Nonetheless, it remained my duty to act as Richard's loyal wife.

"Why didn't you put forth your claim before?" said John de Vere, Earl of Oxford. "It would have saved us a passel of trouble had you spoken up."

Richard flushed. "Though truth for a time may rest and be put to silence," he replied, "yet it never dies."

"Humph," snorted Oxford.

"My lords," said Viscount Henry Bourchier and Richard's brother-in-law. "Should we not discuss this now? Duke Richard has presented his case, and furnished his genealogy. I suggest we take some time to study it."

Voices murmured and robes swished as the lords peered at Richard's parchment.

"This claim is a nothing," sneered Nan's husband, Exeter. "It derives through a woman. And we know women are good for only one thing." He laughed.

My lips thinned as I glared. Being so close to him, and having his vulgar remarks shoved into my face, made me physically sick. How was Nan? I knew only she'd given her lord one daughter some five years before. My anger welled up and veered rapidly from Exeter to Richard, and back again. Like a weathervane in a storm.

"My lord of York's claim is derived from his lady mother, Anne de Mortimer," said Bourchier.

"But the whole claim is dominated by females," objected Somerset, fingering the parchment. As the son of Richard's greatest enemy, Henry Somerset was the last person who wanted to see Richard's claim prevail. "Look at this." He pointed with his finger. "Not only is the claim though his mother Anne de Mortimer, but also though his great-grandmother Philippa, daughter of Lionel of Antwerp."

"His claim would be far stronger if it were through the male line," said Northumberland.

"Like that of our lord king," chimed in Somerset.

Richard glared but was prevented from speaking by Bourchier. "Women may inherit, my lords."

He looked at Norfolk in appeal. Norfolk's opinion carried weight.

"When there is no male heir, then yes, a woman may inherit," said Norfolk. He'd been studying the parchment intently, and now he took off his eyeglasses and shook his head slowly. "I am sorry to say this, my lords, but indeed I think my lord of York has the better claim."

Richard beamed.

There was a roar of disapproval.

Richard went white.

My heart sank. Just as I feared, Richard did not have the support he needed. The better claim to the throne didn't matter—his enemies would fight him tooth and claw.

"We cannot change horses in midstream," said Northumberland.

"It's unthinkable to renege on our oaths of allegiance," said Oxford.

"York cannot be King," shouted Somerset.

"My lords, my lords," interrupted Bourchier. "Some compromise must be possible." He looked at Norfolk.

"We could disinherit Prince Édouard," said Norfolk slowly, "and make York heir-apparent."

"That way, York could succeed on the king's death," remarked Exeter with a sneer.

That was not what Richard wanted; ten years older than the king, he was likely to die sooner.

Chapter 6
November 1460 to January 1461

On the eighth day of November, in the year 1460, Richard was proclaimed heir-apparent to the throne and Protector of England by the *Act of Accord.* All the lords, spiritual and temporal, swore allegiance to him as the king's heir, and he in turn swore allegiance to Henry of Lancaster and the lords, saying he would abide by all conventions and compacts. Richard of York now ruled England in the name of the king.

I sat by his side at the Palace of Westminster and endured the uneasy atmosphere of a court torn by factions. Richard seemed to believe his position invincible. But I couldn't sleep at nights. From the north, news was not good.

Marguerite reached a settlement with the Queen of Scotland, and was resting at Falkirk when news of the *Act of Accord* broke. Furious her son had been disinherited, she amassed an army of some twenty thousand men. She acted so swiftly Richard realized what happened only too late. That November, at York, Queen Marguerite challenged Richard to settle the issue of succession by a contest of arms, then marched her army south.

Richard sent my son Edward to Ludlow to repair the damage done by the raid of 1459. Then with Rutland and Salisbury, he marched out of London on the ninth day of December at the head of an army of around six thousand men to meet the queen, leaving Warwick in charge of London.

I settled down to celebrate Christmas with my three youngest children, making many visits to Warwick's residence on the Strand. There we enjoyed the hospitality of his wife Anne and two daughters Bella and Nanette. I allowed myself a much-needed respite, relaxing at Warwick's well-appointed house, surrounded by the good wishes of the London merchants and the people of London. I was grateful that Bella and Nanette were good companions for my boys. Even eight-year-old Richard managed a shy smile when his four-year-old cousin Nanette greeted him. He sat down and began to teach her chess.

"She's too young for that," exclaimed George, who was now eleven. His mouth crammed full of fruit, George held out a sticky hand.

"Come, Bella," he said to his nine-year-old cousin. "Let me show you the steps to the latest dance."

I smiled at the handsome pair they made. My children were happy. I should try to be so, for their sake.

"I miss Father," whispered fourteen-year-old Margaret, sitting down beside me.

I covered her cold fingers with my own. "So do I," I replied, looking at the thick snow falling outside. I shivered at the thought of Richard having to endure that cold. "Let us pray that he finds some peace and joy this Christmastide."

❦

"Your lord is gone, madam," said the messenger, crossing himself.

"You say he was cut down?" I took a shaky breath.

"He was pulled off his horse."

My hands flew to my mouth to prevent shrieks, for I didn't want the children to hear.

Everything went black.

❦

When I came to, I was bewildered to find myself in my bedchamber in the middle of the day.

Jenet wiped my face with a lavender-scented handkerchief. "You've had a nasty shock, my lady."

I gazed up into her brown eyes. "Is it true?"

Jenet nodded.

I looked away. Only forty-nine. If only I'd loved him as he deserved. He'd never had an easy life. Orphaned by the time he was four. Then he married me—

By the time Richard reached Sandal Castle in Yorkshire, the poor weather left few supplies. He spent Christmas there and, shortly afterwards, sent a party of men to forage. They were ambushed by Lancastrian scouts. On hearing of this, my lord of York rode out of Sandal Castle with Salisbury and Rutland in a heroic effort to protect his men. The whole Lancastrian army surrounded him. They pulled him off his horse, and murdered him. Salisbury was killed during the ensuing battle. Rutland was murdered in cold blood after the battle ended. He was only seventeen years old.

As the truth of what had happened dribbled into my mind, I became ill. I sobbed for days as my heart squeezed out drops of guilt and pity. Only after my tears dried did my anger surface. Why had he impulsively rushed out of the castle? Didn't he have scouts who could tell him that a whole army was waiting to cut him to pieces? His stupidity cost not only his life, but those of our son Rutland and my beloved brother Salisbury.

But he'd done his duty, I wept one night as his face floated before me. He couldn't let his men be cut down without trying to save them. And people respected him for that, extolling his knightly virtues whenever they came to console me.

"I'll make it up to you, my love," I murmured into a pillow.

Over the years, at the Augustinian priory at Clare in Suffolk, I erected a shrine to my lord of York in the form of a repository of documents and other memorabilia commemorating his life. I built an image of the lost heroic father, the worthy statesman, the pious man chosen by God to be king, and the courageous warrior beleaguered by his enemies. It was imperative that the House of York pull together to fight its enemies. And folk needed a hero to inspire.

And so my marriage came to an end. But I did not have the luxury of grieving forever, for there was a war on.

After a month, I sat up in bed and took a deep breath. I was free. As a fabulously wealthy woman, I could live in comfort for the rest of my days. There would be no more pregnancies. I could indulge my slightest whim. And best of all, I need never marry again, for I was far too powerful to be cozened by an ambitious aristocrat seeking to feather his nest. I closed my eyes and silently thanked Our Blessed Lady.

Chapter 7
February to March 1461

After the massacre at Sandal Castle, Edward gathered the Yorkist forces together and fought a battle at Mortimer's Cross, which he won on the Feast of Candlemas, the second day of February in 1461, just a month after Richard was murdered.

The main part of the Lancastrian army moved south, marching toward London via Grantham, Stamford, Peterborough, Huntingdon, Royston, and Saint Albans. My lady queen was unable to pay her soldiers, so she gave them license to loot. They robbed, burned, raped, and pillaged their way through the countryside. They sacked priories and abbeys. They burned whole villages, barns, and manor houses. Many people fled south from the wrath of the northerners, carrying with them dreadful tales of atrocities. These reports caused many towns to switch sides, furthering the Yorkist cause.

On the twelfth day of February, Warwick rode out of London at the head of a large army, making his way north. He met the queen's army at Saint Albans on the seventeenth. Thus the Second Battle of Saint Albans commenced. Warwick would have won this engagement but for the treachery of one commander who held back, then raced to join the Lancastrian side. Under the cover of darkness, Warwick gathered up the remnants of his army and marched west to meet Edward of York.

As news of Warwick's defeat reached London, panic spread. Streets emptied as merchants shut and locked their shops. Folk barricaded themselves inside their houses. Some wealthy merchants even went abroad. The queen sent a deputation to London's mayor to negotiate the terms of the capital's surrender. She ordered the Londoners to proclaim Edward of York a traitor and assured them of amnesty.

The Londoners did not trust her.

My lady queen countered by sending four hundred of her elite troops to march on Aldgate, where they demanded admittance to the city.

The people of Aldgate barred their entry.

Another group of the queen's men made it to Westminster, but were driven away by the indignant Londoners. And so the queen retreated to Dunstable in Bedfordshire, some forty miles to the northwest.

I was staying at my London residence of Baynard's Castle, increasingly concerned that George and Richard might be taken hostage for Edward's good behavior. Early one morning, I put them on a ship bound for Burgundy, where they would remain under the protection of Duke Philip until it was safe for them to return. Margaret remained in London with me, and every day we went from house to house, accepting hospitality from the good folk of London while persuading them to stay with the Yorkist cause despite the terrifying tales they were hearing about the queen's army.

On February 27, Edward rode into London at the head of twenty thousand knights and thirty thousand foot soldiers. I was reading in my solar at Baynard's Castle when the roar of the crowd reached my ears. I rose and went to my *prie-dieu* to pray. When I rose, the shouts of the crowd had become more distinct.

"Hail to the Rose of Rouen," they roared. One imaginative young man sang:

Let us walk in a new vineyard,
and let us make a gay garden into the month of March,
with this fair white rose and herb,
the Earl of March.

Smiling, I walked outside with Margaret. Edward was here, the Londoners behind him.

"Mother!" he exclaimed, vaulting off his gelding. "My fair sister!"

"Well met, my son," I said loudly and clearly so that the crowd could understand. I had not seen Edward since the death of Richard. Now, he was the head of the House of York. Nearly nineteen, he cut a striking figure, and he held the Londoners in the palm of his hand. With him was his cousin Warwick, already beloved of the people.

"Greetings, dear nephew," I said, kissing Warwick's cheek. Warwick was an ambitious, proud aristocrat who wanted to serve as the king's chief minister, but he had no thoughts of being king himself. As the grandson of Joan de Beaufort, born of an adulterous relationship between John of Gaunt and Catrine de Roet, Warwick did not have a tenable claim to the throne. And so, he supported his cousin Edward.

We waved to the crowd, then I took them inside for mulled wine and counsel, which I invited Margaret to attend, believing she should understand matters of state.

The discussion was not congratulatory. Edward's position was not strong. Technically, he was an attainted traitor. He lacked funds, as well as the support of the majority of the magnates.

"It is imperative that you have the support of the London merchants," I remarked.

"Don't worry, Mother. We'll test the waters first," said Edward, kissing my cheek.

Chapter 8
Saint John's Fields, London
Sunday, March 1, 1461

For the first time in a long time, it was safe enough to go out, and the Londoners wanted to see the army defending them from the marauding Lancastrians. After morning Mass, they poured out of the northern edge of the city toward Saint John's Fields, where the Yorkist army camped.

It was a cool, blustery day with the wind whipping the ladies' veils around their faces. Fine ladies huddled in their mounds of sables, while their less well-off neighbors donned thick, woolen mantles. Warwick vaulted off his horse and strode among them, basking in their affection and warmth, the Bishop of London at his side. Someone even found a couple of wooden boxes for him to stand on, so that he could be seen by all.

"Good people of London!" he exclaimed. "You may want to know why I say that King Henry is a usurper."

The crowd laughed and inched closer.

"It's simple," remarked Warwick. "My cousin Edward is descended from Edward III's second son, while Henry of Lancaster is descended from Edward III's third son."

"What happened to Edward III's first son?" someone asked.

"A goodly question," replied Warwick. "Edward III's first son had an only child, who became King Richard II. But King Richard had no children, and so his line died out."

"So you are saying that the Earl of March is the legitimate heir to the throne?" asked a well-dressed young man, wearing a thick mantle of beaver fur.

"Exactly, my friend," replied Warwick. He turned to the Bishop of London.

"Good people," intoned the bishop, "we want to know your opinion. Think you that Edward, Earl of March, should be King of England?"

"Yea! Yea! King Edward!" shouted the crowd, clapping their hands.

The soldiers of the Yorkist army accompanied this acclamation by drubbing on their armor.

❦

"We must call a council, here at Baynard's Castle," I said, when Warwick returned bringing news of what happened in Saint John's Fields. Certainly, events proceeded apace and it was best to strike while the iron was hot.

"We must invite the Archbishop of Canterbury, all the bishops, and all of the peers. Parliament is in session, so it will be an easy matter to manage. I will have the invitations sent out now."

I snapped my fingers, sending people in all directions.

On the third day of March, the magnates present at the meeting that I convened at Baynard's Castle agreed that Edward should be offered the throne.

Still, I couldn't sleep that night. How was it that everything Richard had striven for so mightily was dropping into Edward's lap? The people of London scarcely knew him, yet they'd taken him to their hearts. Was it out of respect for the late duke?

I felt a twinge of guilt, then quickly suppressed it. Since Marguerite did not feel guilty about her illegitimate son, why should I? Richard was in heaven, and nothing could hurt him now. Clearly no one knew that Edward was not the duke's son, not even Edward himself. I vowed to keep it that way.

❦

Next morning, Warwick was ushered in just as I was breaking my fast.

"I come with a petition, dear Aunt!" he cried in ringing tones.

I rose, thanking Our Blessed Lady that my sleeplessness of the night before had caused me to rise early and put on my finest attire. Behind Warwick was a crowd of familiar faces. This could only be a deputation from the

Lords and the Commons. I beckoned to my steward. "Ask Lord Edward to come at once."

When Edward walked in around an hour later, he looked every inch a king. I regarded him with astonishment, feeling again that now-familiar quandary that Blaybourne used to put me in—that a peasant could look like an aristocrat.

"God Save King Edward," raised a faint voice.

I turned around.

"'Tis the crowd outside," remarked Warwick. "They followed me all the way from the Herber and have been waiting."

I smiled. "Let us open the door, therefore, that we may hear them."

"King Edward! God Save King Edward!" chanted the crowd outside, as my steward slowly opened the heavy oak door.

My chest swelled as tears pricked.

Warwick went down on one knee. "We humbly beg you, Edward, Earl of March, to accept the crown and royal dignity of England."

Wasn't it fortunate that I named him *Edward*? His name reminded everyone of his descent from King Edward III.

"Aye!" exclaimed the Lords and the Commons. "We beg you to accept the crown."

"Avenge us on King Henry and his wife!" chanted the crowd outside.

Edward bestowed his dazzling smile on everyone and made a pretty speech, in which he accepted their petition.

❦

Warwick summoned London's leading citizens to Saint Paul's Cathedral, where they enthusiastically acclaimed their new sovereign. Truly, Edward behaved like a king that day. He made a thanksgiving offering to God, then processed to Westminster Hall where he took the oath of the new monarch.

I found it all I could do to keep from weeping, my son attired in royal robes and the cap of estate, enthroned on the king's bench to the cheers of the greatest magnates of the realm.

Afterwards, everyone formed up in procession and went past delirious Londoners who threw snowdrops and wintergreens at their new sovereign. They went to Westminster Abbey, where the abbot and monks presented Edward with the crown and scepter of Saint Edward the Confessor. Edward made offerings at the high altar and the Confessors Shrine before seating himself in the coronation chair. He addressed the congregation, explaining to them why he was their rightful king. When the lords asked the people if they would have Edward as their king, their roars were loud enough to lift the roof. The magnates then knelt, one by one, to do homage to Edward, while the monks sang the *Te Deum.*

On the thirteenth day of March, Edward left for the north.

Chapter 9
Baynard's Castle, London
April 3rd 1461

On the third day of April, I received a letter from Edward. I called my household together and read it to them from the steps of the dais of Baynard Castle's great hall.

Well-beloved Mother, we greet you well. It has pleased God to grant us a great victory at Towton this twenty-ninth day of March, in the first year of our reign. We now advance on London, where I shall soon greet you in person.

"Edward the King!" Cups and tankards clanked and everyone toasted my son. The noise they made carried outside, and an excited crowd gathered. I ordered my steward to proclaim the news of Edward's victory and provide a cup of ale for anyone who wanted to toast him. Then I mounted the stairs to my bedchamber to read the rest of the letter.

On the twenty-eighth day of March, I sent Cousin Warwick to secure the bridge over the River Aire, but we were ambushed, and many of our number were killed. Cousin Warwick was wounded in the leg, but it was just a graze. When the news spread, the soldiers were full dismayed. But Cousin Warwick saved the day by killing his own horse, in full view of the army. He told them that he would fight on foot and die with his men, rather than yield another inch.

I lay back against my pillows. How proud my father would have been to see how indispensable the Nevilles had become to the House of York. Just as Salisbury had supported my lord, so now his son Warwick supported my son.

Though the Lancastrians destroyed the bridge, we managed to cross the Aire and set up camp that night on the other bank. Did I forget to mention that the weather was atrocious? My men had to endure driving snow and hail. Baron John de Clifford, whom you well know was responsible for brother Rutland's murder, died.

I shivered and crossed myself, trying not to think of another bitter winter day when my son, husband, and brother had been cut down by those Lancastrian beasts.

> *That night, I stayed in Pontefract castle. The next day, I drew my men up in battle formation near unto the village of Towton. We fought all day long, from around eleven in the morning, to well past compline, in the midst of a thick blizzard. As dusk came on, Norfolk sent in a strong force, and the Lancastrians fled in a rout. Maybe forty thousand souls perished that day, the bloodiest day on English soul. I have given the gravediggers extra wages, for their labor will be long and hard.*

I crossed myself and murmured a prayer. How like Edward to remember the common folk. My heart swelled; he had endured a hard and bitter fight, and he had won. Now, I would be able to summon George and Richard home from their exile in Burgundy.

> *Written at Towton, the thirtieth day of March, by your most loving son,*
>
> *Edwardus Rex.*

❦

A month before his nineteenth birthday, Edward became King of England, styling himself *Edward IV*. Henry of Lancaster and Marguerite d'Anjou were in York when they heard the news of their defeat. They fled north. Exeter was in their train.

Edward had won an important victory, yet it was incomplete. Henry of Lancaster, his wife, and her son were still at large, Marguerite vowing she would be revenged on the House of York.

Chapter 10
April to November 1461

Throughout April and May of 1461, I received numerous letters from Edward telling me of his affairs.

Well-Beloved Mother,

I write to you from the fair city of York, where I shall rest to celebrate Easter. My first act on arriving was to order the decent burial of my beloved father, uncle and brother. I hope, dearest Mother, this will give you some peace...

I felt the now familiar rise of bile at the hideous way my menfolk had been treated. I retreated to the privy.

After murdering them, the Lancastrian beasts struck their heads off their bodies and put them atop pikes above Micklegate Bar, the main gateway into the city of York. These beasts even put a paper crown on my lord's severed head before moving off.

Later, propped up in bed with a cup of Jenet's soothing mint potion, I read the rest of the letter.

We are to set off north tomorrow in pursuit of the Bitch of Anjou. My scouts tell me she is making her way towards Scotland with her family...

In early May, Edward left the north and returned to London, where he received a hero's welcome for saving the city from the savagery of the northerners. Unfortunately, he was unsuccessful in preventing the Bitch of Anjou, Henry of Lancaster, and others from reaching refuge in Scotland.

On the twenty-eighth day of June, in the year 1461, Edward was crowned in Westminster Abbey. On that day, he made his younger brother George the Duke of Clarence. Richard was allowed to remain under my care.

I was determined to do something for my eldest daughter Nan. When Marguerite d'Anjou and Henry of Lancaster fled north into Scotland, Exeter had followed, leaving his wife and daughter behind. Edward declared him to be a traitor, and in the normal course of affairs would have confiscated his lands. Yet he offered to restore Exeter's lands to Nan that she might live comfortably for the rest of her life and provide for her daughter, who would now be a wealthy heiress.

Nan was at first unwilling to agree, certain that her husband would eventually return. She gave in only after seeing Edward's coronation. I wanted her to stay awhile in Baynard's Castle, but Nan refused.

"I must manage my lands, madam," she told me. "There are many out there who would take Anne's inheritance away. I must ensure that does not happen."

I could not fault her reasoning. Nan was like a whipped horse. Only time and the greatest patience would enable her to trust anyone again.

❦

On the thirty-first day of July, Edward appointed Warwick to be Warden of the East and West marches on the northern border, thus combining the Percy's share of the defense with that of the Nevilles, for the Percy Earls of Northumberland were Lancastrian still. This was a rich and well-deserved reward for the cousin who'd proved himself a loyal friend. Edward also made him chief advisor, giving him the responsibility of defending the kingdom and of foreign policy.

Not more than a month passed after Edward's coronation before King Charles VII of France died. He was succeeded by his son Louis, who had been friendly towards the Yorkists. But matters between the new kings of England and France did not proceed smoothly. One September day, Edward was closeted in his study with his cousin Warwick, tackling the numerous problems facing England, when a young man flew in and bent at the knee, sweat pouring down his face.

"My lord King: I have here a letter to the queen." He paused and flushed red. "Pardon me, I mean Marguerite of Lancaster."

Warwick swung around. He cut a magnificent figure in a tunic of red velvet, a cloak of purple draped elegantly over one shoulder. "A letter?" he snapped.

"Yes, Your Grace. I mean, your lordship. I'm sorry, good sirs, my wits are that addled—" He gasped for breath.

Edward came forward. At six feet four inches, he was about six inches taller than his cousin. He also dressed magnificently. Today he was wearing a blue satin tunic, slashed to reveal a silver silk undershirt. He placed a large hand on the messenger's shoulder.

"Take a breath, my good man. You look as if you've run all the way from Scotland." He called to his squire. "Bring a cup of ale for this good fellow."

"That's very kind of you sir, I mean, my lord, Your Grace—"

"What is your message?" snapped Warwick, his grey eyes hardening. Now in his early thirties, his fair hair was beginning to grey, and he had lines of experience around his mouth and eyes.

Edward smiled gently and patted the messenger again.

"Have some ale, and tell us how you came by this letter."

"One of your spies intercepted it," replied the messenger, quaffing his ale.

Edward held his hand out and scanned the letter.

Madam, fear not, but be of good comfort, for we have been summoned to see King Louis. Therefore, beware ye venture not your person by sea till ye have other word from us—

Edward glanced up as Warwick came forward. His young unlined face showed little emotion, save for a clenching of the jaw. Silently, he handed over the letter.

"Christ's bones!" exclaimed Warwick. "I thought we had the favor of the new King of France. It is said he hates the House of Anjou. But that doesn't stop her from seeking his aid."

Edward moved to the table in the middle of the room and unrolled a large map that showed England, Scotland, Wales, and France. "We could be invaded at any time," he remarked. "Where do you think she's likely to strike?"

Warwick motioned for the messenger to leave and pointed to the Cotetin peninsula of Normandy. "Her plan might be to try and capture the Channel Isles to make a bridgehead to England from France."

"At the moment, she's in Scotland," replied Edward. "She can only attack the Channel Isles if she's in France. And that depends on King Louis giving her money."

"I have it on good authority that she's already exhausted her own funds. That letter can mean only one thing."

Edward looked up.

"She's worn out her welcome at the Scottish court," remarked Warwick.

Edward frowned. "She might strike from the north."

"Aye, she might," agreed Warwick, rubbing his chin. "All we need is more unrest there."

"Therefore, I think that you, cousin, should march to Alnwick," said Edward, pointing to the far north of England, "and capture it."

"Right," said Warwick, nodding. "I'll go there forthwith. We cannot have the Bitch of Anjou take a major Northumbrian stronghold."

He bowed and disappeared, followed by his large train of retainers, all bearing his badge of the staff and ragged bear on scarlet tunics.

❦

Warwick captured not only Alnwick but also Bamburgh Castle, thus ensuring that the new king had the most important Northumbrian strongholds to serve as a bulwark against any invasion from Scotland.

On November 1st 1461, Edward opened his first parliament. On that day, he made his youngest brother Richard Duke of Gloucester and sent him to live at Middleham, with my blessing, to train as a knight under Warwick's supervision.

Chapter 11
Summer 1463

The crowning of my son Edward seemed to be a vindication for all the sacrifices made. I was given my lands back and admitted to the highest councils of the land. Folk said that Duchess Cecylee ruled the king as she pleased. Never before had a lady had such influence, unless you counted the activities of Queen Alainor of Aquitaine of three centuries before. No more would England have to endure a warrior queen who struck terror into the hearts of men with a rampaging army of animals she was unable to control. Instead, I modeled myself on Queen Alainor, known for her fair dealing whenever she dispensed justice at the various assizes held around the country.

In all of this, I was ably assisted by my nephew Warwick. And yet this was a time of peril for the new king, for the Bitch of Anjou was creating havoc, both by negotiating with the French and Burgundian princes and by repeatedly taking the Northumbrian fortresses. Finally, Warwick arranged a peace conference between Edward, King Louis XI of France, and Duke Philip of Burgundy in the summer of 1463. The objective was to close France and Burgundy to Marguerite d'Anjou and Henry of Lancaster.

After that, Warwick set about finding a suitable bride for Edward, for in the two years he had been king he'd not had time to think about this matter.

"The Duke of Burgundy has offered his two nieces," I remarked, "Lady Marguerite de Bourbon and her sister Jeanne."

"How old are these ladies?" asked Warwick.

"Lady Marguerite has twenty-four years. Lady Jeanne, her sister, is a little younger. She has twenty-one years."

Warwick steepled his fingers as he leaned back in his elaborately carved chair. How he reveled in his power and influence. Indeed, in those days, Warwick appeared to have so much power that folk called him *The Kingmaker*. Or as one wit at the French court put it: "They have but two rulers in England, Monsieur de Warwick and another whose name I have forgotten." At that moment he was securing the northern border, negotiating with the French and Burgundians, and helping Edward sort out the country's finances and judicial system. He strode about, followed by his huge army of retainers, always busy, always preoccupied.

"Edward has now twenty-one years," he remarked. "He might be happier with someone younger."

I nodded. "Perhaps you are right. There is a younger lady with whom I have been in correspondence. Lady Isabella of Castile has now turned twelve. She is very suitable, for she is the half-sister of King Henry of Castile and possible heiress to the throne of Castile."

"What of Lady Bona of Savoy?"

My ears pricked up, as an image of Blaybourne dressed in his finery materialized. I was now so confused about the swirl of events surrounding my lover, that I knew not whether he was a humble archer, a scholar, or a nobleman called Philippe of Savoy.

"Tell me about her."

"She is sister to the Queen of France. Her father is Duke Louis of Savoy, the eldest son of Duke Amadeus of Savoy."

Since Richard's death, I'd made discreet inquiries and learned that Philippe of Savoy was the youngest son of Duke Amadeus. Strangely, he remained unmarried. Lady Bona would be his niece, and thus a possible cousin to Edward.

"She is a little older than Princess Isabella," continued Warwick, "and would now be turning fourteen."

"She would be able to bear Edward sons sooner. But what are the political implications?"

"This match would close France to the Lancastrian exiles," replied Warwick. "As we speak, the Lancastrian usurper Henry is at large in Scotland, while the Bitch of Anjou and her son Édouard are in Burgundy, pleading for the Duke to give them succor."

"We should do something about that."

Warwick smiled. "We need do nothing, dear Aunt, providing that France is on our side. It is King Louis's ambition to crush Burgundy. And he will succeed. He's crafty and wily, and France is a much greater power than Burgundy."

"That may be so," I replied. "But is Louis trustworthy? King Henry of Castile is weak and therefore malleable. I have it on good authority that he would be pleased to marry off his half-sister Isabella to a foreign power, for he has a newborn daughter to think of and the Lady Isabella is her rival for the throne. I believe he would agree to very acceptable terms."

The door opened and Edward suddenly appeared. "Mother," he said. "What are you discussing?"

"Your marriage," I replied, smiling up at him. He was my golden boy with his unusual height, thick head of golden hair, and bright blue eyes.

"We were just talking of two promising young ladies," said Warwick. "Isabella of Castile and Bona of Savoy."

"And what do these ladies look like?"

"Lady Isabella is highly intelligent and pleasing to look at," I replied, making a mental note to obtain a portrait of her. Of course Edward would want an attractive wife.

"Does she have violet eyes?" asked Edward. "Or hair the color of silver?"

There was only one person who met that description, and that was Lady Eleanor Talbot, the youngest daughter of my dearest friend Margaret and now Lady Butler. She'd been married years ago.

Warwick looked at Edward intently. "Do you have someone in mind?"

Edward shrugged and smiled.

I waited for him to speak, a strange sensation of unease crawling up my spine.

"Do not look so serious, Mother," said Edward finally. "I wish only for a beauty."

"And that you shall have," declared Warwick, rising and slapping him on the back. "I have already turned down two ladies your mother suggested on the grounds they were too old."

Edward grimaced.

"I understand your tastes," said Warwick. He glanced at me and forbore to say more.

I thinned my lips. It was greatly disquieting that every young woman in the land was flinging herself at Edward.

"Find me a bride who is young, lively and very beautiful," said Edward, clasping Warwick's hand. And with a quick kiss on my cheek, he disappeared.

Chapter 12
The Abbey of Our Lady and Saint John the Evangelist
Reading, Berkshire
September 14, 1464

Knowing that my son had chosen for his motto *Confort et Liesse* (*Comfort and Joy*) should have prepared me. For Edward had one fatal flaw, he could be dangerously impulsive.

One fine September day in the Year of Our Lord 1464, I was waiting to talk with him about his forthcoming marriage to the Lady Bona of Savoy when the door to the chapter house burst open and everyone poured out. Edward hurried over.

"What's happened?" I asked, noticing the hubbub and the long faces of his councilors.

"Mother, I am married. I have just told my councilors —"

"Married!" The color drained from my face. "Who is she?"

"You do not know her, Mother. She is Dame Élisabeth Grey."

"*Dame* Grey. You mean she was married before?"

"Yes," he replied.

My stomach lurched and I staggered.

Edward signaled to hovering servants to bring me a chair and some wine. At another signal, everyone left. I sat and sipped my wine slowly while marshaling my swirling thoughts. Eventually, I looked up at Edward. "Who are her parents?"

"Her mother is Jacquetta of Luxembourg, the daughter of the Count of St. Pol."

I knew that name—it could not be. "Her father?"

"Earl Rivers."

"You mean that jumped-up squire Sir Richard Woodville," I snapped, "Sir Nobody."

Edward winced.

I knew who Dame Élisabeth Grey was. Her mother Jacquetta had created a scandal nearly thirty years before when, as the widowed Duchess of Bedford and aunt-by-marriage to the king, she had married Sir Richard Woodville shortly after her husband's death. Sir Richard was far below her in rank and only had his good looks to commend him.

As for Dame Grey, that doll-like child now had gilt-gold hair, pointed features, and a sly smile. She was a year older than my beloved daughter Joan would have been, had she lived, which meant that at twenty-seven, she was five years *older* than Edward. She was the widow of a Lancastrian knight who'd fought against us in the recent wars—Sir John Grey of Groby. She had two boys. She was poor. She had a large number of relatives. In short, she had nothing to recommend her. Moreover, she and her mother had interfered the day of Marguerite's churching, the day I struggled to have Nan come home to me. I turned on Edward.

"How could you be such a fool?"

He flinched.

"How long have you been married?"

He flushed and the silence held. Finally he lifted his chin and looked at me squarely. "Since May."

"Since *May*? Edward, that cannot be so."

There was silence again.

"Are you saying you have been married for the past *four months*?"

"Yes, Mother."

"Why didn't you tell me?"

He hung his head. A flush crept up his neck.

I sagged in my seat. If only I'd been allowed to spend time with Edward when he was growing up. If only Richard hadn't taken him away.

"Edward," I said, "I am devoted to you, you know that. I have worked tirelessly for you all my life. Why could you not confide in me, your own mother?"

"I knew you would talk me out of it."

I looked at him steadily for a moment. He was a coward, as well as completely irresponsible. "Do you truly think she is suitable?"

"Yes."

I picked up my wine-cup. "The fact that you have been married for four months and have told no one will indicate to everyone *you* do not think her to be suitable."

"She is the most beautiful woman in England."

"I'm glad you think so." I put my wine-cup down. "Did the wedding occur in a church?"

He shook his head.

"Who were the witnesses?"

"Élisabeth came with her mother. There was the priest."

I gazed at him. It was like his christening, that underhanded affair in a private chapel away from prying eyes.

"That was a very private ceremony," I murmured eventually. "I was planning a magnificent celebration for you, my son, something that would befit a King of England. I was hoping to meet your bride beforehand, to welcome her into the family."

Edward took my hand in his. "And you will know Élisabeth," he said. "Mother, I would like you to befriend her."

I stared at him and withdrew my hand.

"How well do you know her?"

"I have been courting her for several months."

I tapped the arm of my chair to control my surging feelings. My golden boy had just crushed all my hopes and dreams. "There are many reasons to marry," I said. "If you had to marry for love, could you not have chosen someone who you had serious reason to believe would make you happy?"

"She does make me happy."

"How?"

He flushed.

I drained my cup of wine. "Remember, Edward, you have a soul to keep. Your wife will have a great deal of power over you."

"She is sweet and charming."

"She wants to be Queen of England."

Edward fiddled with his ring.

"She will not make you happy. Apart from that, there are political reasons for not marrying her."

I rose and stood stiff and tall.

"When you succeeded my lord of York as head of the family, you assumed certain duties and responsibilities. You are now king, and it is the king's duty—for the sake of his family and his country—to marry into a noble or royal house from the continent to enhance his status and increase his possessions. Your cousin has traveled to France on your behalf, and negotiations for your marriage to Bona of Savoy are now far advanced."

"Cousin Warwick will accept my marriage."

I raised an eyebrow: "You didn't confide in your cousin?"

Edward was silent.

I folded my arms. "It is the height of folly to antagonize the Earl of Warwick so unnecessarily. Why he was expecting to conclude these marriage negotiations within the month."

Edward twisted his signet ring again.

"As you know, I have also been in correspondence with Isabella of Castile, in case the French marriage negotiations broke down. Either of these princesses would have been fit to be your queen."

"But I don't know them," protested Edward. "What makes you think they would have made me happy?"

"They are young," I ticked my fingers. "Bona has fifteen years, and Isabella has thirteen. They are schooled to be queens, having lived their lives in the finest courts of Europe, and it was my hope, as your mother, to train them myself. I wanted to tell them about you, I wanted to mold them to English life, and to the ways of your life. I wanted to supervise their religious instruction and to educate them in literature and the arts, the way my mother did."

"Mother!"

I glared. "I would have ensured they had your best interests at heart."

There was silence.

I had said everything I could. Was there any way of annulling this ridiculous marriage?

But Edward said nothing.

"It is wholly inappropriate," I remarked, staring at his downcast eyes and shut-in face, "for a monarch to marry his own subject where no honor or lands can be gained by it. A rich man marries his maid only for a little easy pleasure. In such marriages, folk admire the maid's good fortune, but think her master lacks judgment. And in this matter, there is no difference so great between any master and maid in this land as between you and this widow."

I paused.

Edward did not react.

"And the fact that she *is* a widow makes everything much worse."

Edward lifted his chin and stared at me.

I gazed back. There was a long silence. Finally I snapped, "This marriage is a blemish and a disparagement to the majesty of a prince!"

I swept out.

Chapter 13
Westminster Palace, London
Feast of Saint Lucy
December 13, 1464

It was as if I'd never spoken.

Later that September at Michaelmas, Dame Élisabeth Grey was escorted into Reading Abbey by Warwick and George. The Serpent was presented to the magnates and the people as their Sovereign Lady, and the whole assembly of people knelt to do her honor.

Except for myself.

I could not submit.

I made my displeasure clear by being absent.

My absence was noted by everyone.

Edward had disgraced himself with this awful marriage. In turn, I styled myself *Queen by Right.*

From then on, there were two queens at Edward's court. I remained in the queen's apartments, and Edward was forced to build a special wing onto one of his palaces to accommodate the Serpent and her entourage. Shortly after her elevation, she got her revenge in the most predictable way. The horde of poverty-stricken relatives descended on the court and proceeded to elbow their way into the aristocracy. I enumerate as follows.

Item: Margaret Woodville, sister to the Serpent, married October 1464 to Thomas Fitzalan, Baron Maltravers, the Earl of Arundel's heir.

Item: Catherine Woodville, sister to the Serpent, married April 1465 to Henry Stafford, Duke of Buckingham, my sister Anne's grandson.

Item: Martha Woodville, sister, married in June 1465 to Sir John Bromley.

Item: Jacqueline Woodville, sister, married February 1466 to John le Strange, Baron Strange of Knockin.

Item: Thomas Grey, the Serpent's eldest son, married in October 1466 to Nan's daughter, Anne Holland.

Item: Mary Woodville, sister, married January 1467 to William Herbert, Lord Dunster, the Earl of Pembroke's heir.

Item: Eleanor Woodville, sister, married July 1467 to Sir Anthony Grey.

Item: Anne Woodville, sister, married in July 1467 to William, Viscount Bourchier the eldest son of Richard's sister Isabel.

What more need I say?

❦

"Cecylee, Queen by Right, Duchess of York," roared the herald.

There was a stir as I lifted my chin high and sailed into the room. I dressed in my usual dark colors worn since my lord of York's death. This time my gown was midnight-blue velvet, the neck and bodice covered in a white silken scarf, over which I wore a simple white headdress surmounted by a coronet.

Everyone sank like a wave as I approached, the gentlemen bowing, the ladies curtseying. All except for one figure, dressed in cloth of gold brocade with a plunging neckline to set off the emeralds around her neck. The dress formed pools of gold as it flowed around her feet. This figure stood motionless with her back erect as I approached. At the end of that long hall, I found myself finally face-to-face with the Serpent, my daughter-in-law, Edward's wife, and soon-to-be crowned Queen of England.

We stared at each other for several minutes. In that huge hall, thronging with hundreds of people, the silence was deafening. Finally, the Serpent's mouth curved into a smile.

"Well met, Mother!" she cried out, louder than I would have liked, as the room rustled to life. "You are welcome, indeed, to our Christmas Court."

I stiffened as she took my arm, but the Serpent held me in a vice-like grip. I looked around for Edward, but he was nowhere to be seen.

"Edward has been detained," said the Serpent, as she led me along the corridor, followed by her ladies. "In the meantime, I wanted to invite you to my private chambers so that we could have a quiet talk."

As we arrived, the door shut behind us, and the Serpent signaled to her women to pour wine and bring out refreshments. She indicated a seat for me to sit in, but I shook my head.

"As you wish," she remarked, shrugging. And smiling, she sat down.

Her ladies followed suit, some of them smiling behind their hands.

How dare she to sit in my presence?

The Serpent leaned back in her chair and sipped delicately from a crystal goblet that sparkled with gold lights reflecting the gold of her dress. She watched me for a moment. Finally, she spoke.

"Queen by Right," she murmured, twisting the goblet between her fingers so that the reflected colors moved hither and thither. "An interesting title, madam. Did you inherit it from someone in your family?"

I glared at her. The sound of smothered giggles struck my ear. It was followed by shushing sounds.

The Serpent fastened her eyes on her goblet and kept them there until the room was completely quiet. Then she looked at me.

"Has a Queen of England ever ruled through her son?" she asked.

"Yes," said I, raising my chin. "Queen Alainor of Aquitaine, of blessed memory—"

There was a splutter behind my back. I turned to glare in that general direction. When I turned back to the Serpent, she was leaning forward in her chair, her brow furrowing in concentration.

"She was the mother of Richard, Coeur de Lion," I explained.

"I see." The Serpent turned the crystal goblet in her fingers. These goblets had recently come into fashion. Edward had imported them from Venice, at great expense, for the Serpent was determined to emulate the luxury of the court of Burgundy. Even if it meant plunging the Crown into debt.

"Was Richard, Coeur de Lion, actually married?" asked the Serpent.

"His mother found him a suitable bride in the Princess Berengaria of Navarre," I replied.

The Serpent remained in her chair, leaning forward, looking up at me with one eyebrow raised. She held the exquisite goblet poised delicately between the fingers of two hands.

"I see," she said evenly.

Again, there was a splutter behind me.

The Serpent sighed, put her goblet down, rose, and beckoned to someone behind me. Everyone in the room rose also.

A rosy-cheeked giggling child of around six or so jumped out, and after a vain attempt to stifle her giggles, sketched me a very shaky curtsey.

The Serpent smiled. "May I present to you my sweet sister Catherine?" She turned to her sister: "Be off with you, child, for we have serious matters to discuss."

The child giggled and ran off, followed by her governess.

The Serpent turned back to me. "Are you sure you wouldn't rather sit?"

I cleared my throat. "No, I thank you."

The Serpent resumed her seat, and everyone in the room sat down also, leaving me standing.

The Serpent signaled, and a servant rushed forward to refill her crystal goblet. She took a sip, turned to me.

"Now where were we?" she remarked as the room fluttered with sounds of whispers and giggles. "Ah, yes. You were telling me of King Richard's marriage."

I glared at her. "You should not be sitting there, madam. Your family is Lancastrian. You fought against us in the recent war. I lost my husband, son, and brother to Lancastrian beasts who—"

I gulped for air, unable to bear the images that rose up. "You were damsel to the Bitch of Anjou. You are two-faced, madam. You are duplicitous."

"But the time has come to put that behind us."

"I never forget," I replied. "And you should not. Your husband died too."

The Serpent glanced at me, biting her lip. She lowered her eyes and played with her crystal goblet. "Families are so interesting—"

"Indeed," I exclaimed. "Your family, for instance, madam. Your father is a jumped-up nobody, and I understand that you are descended, on your mother's side, from the fay Melusine, the sorceress who vanished in a puff of smoke when forced to attend Mass."

I paused and jabbed my finger at her. "Your wiles, and that of your mother, have entrapped my son, bewitched him, so that he lost his reason and married you."

A hush fell as the Serpent stared at me, her face white. Witchcraft was a serious accusation, and she knew it.

My head high, I turned on my heel and left.

I swept into my chamber, and took breath.

Good.

I had made my feelings clear.

My shoulders relaxed, the bottled-up frustration of the past several months leaking out.

I had just crushed my mortal enemy.

I lost no time in going to see Edward to discuss the evils of his marriage. I pointed out that since there were hardly any witnesses, it would be an easy matter to get it annulled.

He heard me out, then turned to me and smiled. "Madam, I am well content with my lovely wife, and I pray you be content also. Both Élisabeth and I already have children. England will have heirs."

I stared at him, speechless with indignation. It was only then that I realized I did not know my son at all.

Chapter 14
Queen's Apartments, Westminster Palace, London
Feast of The Epiphany
January 6, 1465

To the Steward of Fotheringhay Castle, Northamptonshire,

Greetings.

May it please you to know that Cecylee, Duchess of York, Queen By Right, has come to the end of her stay in London and will be arriving in Fotheringhay in ten days. See to it that all necessary provisions are made against her return.

Given, this sixth day of January, in the Year of Our Lord 1465.

I took this document from my scribe, read it through, and smiled. I intended to use my new title until I could persuade Edward to find another wife. As I congratulated myself on putting the Serpent in her place, the door to my chamber burst open. It was Cath.

"Cis, dearest: I wanted you to be the first to know. I am to marry Sir John Woodville."

Cath was no longer young, for she was sixty-seven years old. Still she was a handsome woman, who would have looked younger had she not lost most of her teeth. Every time she smiled, she drooled.

I handed her my handkerchief and signaled for the scribe to leave. "You mean to tell me, sister, the Serpent has commanded you to marry her brother John?"

Cath threw back her head and laughed: "Fancy calling Edward's queen *The Serpent.* What has she done to you to deserve that name?"

"She has wormed her way into the House of York like a canker eating at an apple. Now she is commanding you to marry her brother."

"He's a lovely young man."

"How old is he?"

"He's—nineteen, I believe she said."

"Cath!"

Cath flushed.

"You know how this is going to look."

"But I'm lonely."

"A lady of your years matched to a callow youth of nineteen."

"But you know how much I like male company—"

"How could you agree to it?"

"—and I've had three husbands taken from me."

"You know folk will not be kind."

"I don't see why I shouldn't marry this charming young man."

"She's trying to humiliate you. The Serpent wants your money. After burying three husbands, she knows you to be wealthy."

"But he's sweet!"

"I'm going to see her now."

"But Cis—" Cath plucked at my sleeve.

I brushed her off. "This isn't about you, Cath. She's trying to humiliate the Nevilles, the House of York, and me. I must put a stop to it."

❦

I came upon the Serpent seated on a gilded chair with her ladies around her. She was embroidering a magnificent altar cloth made of cloth of gold and purple velvet. She wore a silver dress that reflected the blood-red rubies at her throat and on her fingers. She looked up as I entered, but did not rise.

"Good Morrow, Mother." She signaled to her ladies to put the altar cloth away and bring out refreshments in the form of oranges, figs, nuts, and warm spiced wine.

"I wish to talk to you."

"About your sister's forthcoming nuptials?" The Serpent leaned back in her chair as she peeled an orange with a bejeweled dagger. While she talked, the blade flashed as it went in and out, separating the peel from the sweet, luscious fruit within.

"I cannot allow it to happen."

"And what does your sister say?"

I hesitated. The room rustled with the sounds of the ladies' heavy skirts dragging across the Turkish carpets as they went about their duties. Finally, they took up position around their mistress. A sea of staring eyes met mine.

The Serpent paused, holding the dagger balanced between thumb and finger, and studied me for a moment. "Your sister is *older* than you, is she not? Surely old enough to decide her own fate."

A murmur of laughter ran around the room.

"When I told her of my plans, she seemed delighted. As I remember, she called my brother John a *sweet boy*. So I made the old dame happy. What's wrong with that?"

"You know what's wrong."

The Serpent put her dagger down and stared: "My sweet brother is delighted to make your sister happy. Your sister is happy with my choice of bridegroom, so what could *your* objection be?" She paused for a moment, put her hand to her head, and frowned in concentration as her ladies tittered behind their hands.

"It couldn't be my brother's—bloodlines, now could it?"

I glared.

"I believe that the last time I had the pleasure of your company, you described my father as 'jumped up.'"

"I did. I also said—"

"Perhaps it would help, good mother, if I told you more about Maman, my mother."

"*Your* mother? She was the cause of a great scandal. She was the king's aunt, and she married well beneath her."

"I would like to tell you about Maman's family," said the Serpent, handing her cup to one of her ladies and rising. She took my arm.

"My mother has many interesting people she can claim relation with. Surely you know that my mother's father, the Count of St. Pol, was related to the Holy Roman Emperor. Or that my mother's mother was an Italian princess, descended from the Orsinis?"

She turned to look at me. "You look surprised, good mother," she cooed. "I see you did not know that."

The candles flickered as my vision narrowed. I knew her mother Jacquetta, Duchess of Bedford, was of a higher social station than her father, for I remembered well how she would constantly talk of her family in France. But I'd never really believed her connections were so illustrious. Perhaps because it seemed obvious she would exaggerate in an effort to cover up her husband's humble origins.

"Are you not descended from Queen Alainor of Aquitaine?" said the Serpent.

"Indeed I am."

"And would you have been happy if your son, the king, had married one of Queen Alainor's descendants?"

I gripped the back of a chair. If he'd done that, wouldn't everything have been different?

The Serpent turned slightly, the silver dress fanning out across the floor in a curling wave. She smiled.

"You see, Mother, your son was dutiful after all. I also am descended from Queen Alainor."

I glared at her. How like her mother, to exaggerate her claims.

"That's not true."

"Indeed it is. I am descended, by my mother, from Simon de Montfort and his wife, the Lady Eleanor, one of Queen Alainor's granddaughters."

I shook my head, but could not rid myself of a pounding headache.

"So you need have no further worry about allying yourself with the Woodvilles." The Serpent drew her arm through mine and ushered me out of the room. "We are truly blue-blooded. Your sister will be safe with us."

The door closed shut and I was left in a dark corridor. I shivered with cold. The Serpent's family had fought against the House of York in the war. She was responsible for the murder of Richard, of Salisbury, and of Rutland. Her people were the ones who'd put their heads on top of pikes at Micklegate Bar. She should not be Queen of England.

Within the month, Cath was married to the Serpent's brother John. Much sport was had at poor Cath's expense. One wit described her as a *slip of a girl.* Another referred to this sham arrangement as the *Diabolical Marriage.* I was forced to attend the wedding ceremony, which I found humiliating in the extreme. Just as the Serpent had intended.

Chapter 15
Greenwich Palace, London
Feast of Saints Philip & James
May 3, 1465

At nineteen, Margaret was the most beautiful lady at Edward's court. She greatly resembled her dead sister Joan, with her flawless lily-and-rose complexion and chestnut brown tresses. On this birthday, Edward held a feast followed by dancing to celebrate. Margaret stood in a circle with other young folk, following the beat of the drum first left, then right, that accompanied the recorder and dulcimer, while the dancing-master instructed them on the latest dance steps.

I stood in the garden, enjoying the music while I gave directions to Edward's head steward, having taken in hand the lavish preparations for Margaret's feast.

An unpleasantly shrill voice made me turn.

"Nineteen, is she not? 'Tis full time she was married."

As soon as my eyes met the Serpent's, she took my arm. She chose her moment well, for she was in front of hangers-on and had a vice-like grip that was not easy to dislodge.

"My brother Ned would be the perfect match for Margaret," she remarked. "Why, the king, your son, thinks highly of him."

My cheeks warmed as my stomach turned over. Ned Woodville was one of those gentlemen who seem always to be underfoot, dicing, singing, and not doing anything in particular. Why the king had made him Admiral of the Fleet, heaven only knew. Doubtless it had something to do with the Serpent, for he had no qualifications that I could see, having never fought a sea battle in his life. His bleary eyes and late risings rather told me that he led a life given over to debauchery and drink. Unfortunately, Edward seemed to attract many such followers to his court.

"No need to gape, good mother: You have been remiss. Why haven't you married her off before?"

Why indeed? Margaret was my youngest daughter. I could not bear to part with her. Of course, I must one day. But only to someone who was worthy.

The Serpent continued, "'Tis four years since Edward became king. You've had plenty of time to choose a suitor."

"No."

"'Tis true, I tell you. Why, he was crowned king in June of 1461, near unto the Feast Day of Saints Peter and Paul. You cannot tell me your wits are so addled—"

"Out of the question."

"Why?" The Serpent opened her gold-brown eyes wide. "You don't mean to say my brother is not good enough? That is absurd. Your son, the king, has heaped honors on him. I'm sure he would agree to the match."

The ground heaved and the Serpent's voice receded into the distance as she said, "Think on it, good mother, I beseech you. 'Tis time for her to be married. 'Tis full time."

Her mouth widened into a smile as I sank onto the nearest seat.

She left, followed by ladies who did not trouble to hide their smiles.

I must protect Margaret at all costs. Where was Edward?

❦

When I arrived at the king's apartments, Edward was closeted with Warwick.

"We need an alliance with France," said Warwick as I entered.

"But an alliance with Burgundy would bring in more trade," replied Edward.

"It is imperative that we seal a compact with King Louis," said Warwick. "Otherwise, he'll give shelter to the Lancastrians."

"Louis is too slippery to be trusted," remarked Edward, "so he might do anything. But the London merchants need the trade with Burgundy."

He caught sight of me and instantly came forward. "Mother?"

I sank wordlessly onto a seat while Edward waved away Warwick and sent for wine.

"Mother, what's wrong?"

I sipped my wine, playing for time. Now that I was with Edward, I had no clear idea of what to say.

"I've never seen you look so upset, Mother. Whatever has happened?"

My intuition told me not to mention the Serpent by name. On the other hand, discussing Margaret's marriage with Edward when I had not prepared him for this topic of conversation was going to make me look ridiculous. But I had no choice, so I plunged ahead.

"It's about Margaret."

"Margaret?" Edward's brows furrowed. "You do not mean to say she has gone off and married without my permission?"

"Nothing like that. But I am anxious that she marry well, and marry soon."

Edward's blue eyes bore into mine. "Is that all? Why, Mother, you do surprise me. I thought something truly awful had happened."

"Edward, I need your help. Margaret must be married, and married soon."

"All in good time, Mother. Why the rush now?"

I avoided looking at him. "Is there no prince or duke abroad who needs a wife? I would have my Margaret make a splendid international match."

Edward picked up a scroll of paper and began tapping it with his ring finger. "I have received news that the Duke of Burgundy's heir needs a wife. Charles of Charolais was married to Isabelle of Bourbon. The news from Burgundy is that Countess Isabelle has recently died. Now that would be a good match."

"Oh, yes, Edward. That would be just the thing for her."

"But what of your nephew Warwick? He wouldn't be pleased if you supported a Burgundian alliance."

It was true. Warwick and Edward did not go in the same direction regarding England's foreign policy. They were like an ill-yoked pair of mules, with Warwick pulling towards France and Edward pulling towards Burgundy. I had hitherto supported Warwick's efforts in gaining an alliance with France. I felt that I should stand by him after Edward betrayed him by secretly marrying the Serpent. Now, matters were different: I would do anything to save Margaret from a Woodville alliance.

I rose and assured Edward I would deal with Warwick provided Edward gave his solemn oath that he would lose no time in seeing about a marriage between Margaret and Burgundy's heir.

Edward threw back his head and roared with laughter.

"Really, Mother. There's no need to be so anxious. You know I'm very keen on the Burgundian alliance. I assure you, I will do all in my power to see to this match." His eyes bored into mine. "Mother," he remarked. "You have been acting oddly, you know. Am I missing something?"

I smiled as warmly as I could and assured him that standing in the sun had not agreed with me.

Then I hurried back to the garden and spoke to the steward once more about the arrangements for Margaret's birthday feast.

Chapter 16
Greenwich Palace, London
June 1465

The Serpent was crowned Queen of England on Whitsunday, just at the end of May. I did not attend. While I lay in bed, I braced myself for what might follow.

She didn't keep me waiting long.

"Ah, good mother, there you are."

Edward was nowhere to be seen. As usual, I was surrounded by her people. As always, the Serpent took my arm, in her insultingly overly familiar manner.

"I've been meaning to talk to you about Richard," she said as she took me through a tunnel overhung with lilac. Its sweet, almost sickly scent was overpowering.

"Richard? You mean, my son Richard?"

"How old is he now?"

I paused and glared at her. Her ladies stared at me, so I was forced to answer. "He has about twelve years."

"He's growing up," she exclaimed. "We do not have much time."

"What does this have to do with you?"

She smiled. "Ah. Now we come to the point." She took my arm again. "You see, good mother, I have Richard's best interests at heart. Now, Warwick—"

"What about Warwick?" I demanded, drawing my arm away.

"Now, now. There, there." She patted my arm. "There's no need to be *so* suspicious." She pouted, but there was a glint of amusement in her eyes. "I have a plan for Richard." She took my arm again.

I withdrew it and glared.

She smiled and folded her arms. "I think Richard should be moved from Warwick's care to that of my brother. Do you not agree?"

It was the custom for young noblemen, like Richard, to be taken away from their families at the age of seven or eight and sent to train in the arts of war in another household. I had sent my youngest son to be trained in the household of my nephew. However, the Serpent and Warwick loathed each other.

I glared. "Richard is in my keeping."

"He's in Warwick's keeping," she pointed out, "and I do not think Warwick is—satisfactory. Richard would do much better if he were under the care of my brother, Sir Antony Woodville."

I froze. Of all her siblings – and the Serpent had many – Sir Antony was the most widely respected. He was learned, cultured, and had a great reputation on the jousting field.

"What say you, good mother?"

"I have to think of Richard's wishes," I replied. " He has not had an easy childhood and he is happy at Middleham —"

"How strange that the wealthiest peer in the realm, your husband, the Duke of York, should have so many sickly children," she remarked. "Let me see, you had five daughters did you not? But two died." She ticked them off on her fingers. "Joan, the eldest, and Ursula, the youngest. And you had eight sons, did you not, madam? And of those sons, five died. Henry, Edmund, William, John, Thomas. So many sons, so many good fighting men for the House of York. But they died."

"What exactly is your meaning?" I snapped.

The Serpent edged away, making fluttering motions with her hands. "You do frighten me so, Mother dear, when you get angry." She paused and flashed a sidelong smile. "And you do get angry, do you not?"

I compressed my lips. Since the day my father had given me that beating, I had always been angry.

"Maman," she remarked, speaking now of her own mother, "had fifteen children, six sons and nine daughters and they all survived. And she had considerably less money than you. Now, why would that be? Was it all the riding around you did when you should have been confined to one of your husband's castles, awaiting the birth of his children?"

I made a wall of silence between us.

"They do say," continued the Serpent, putting her hand on the gnarled bole of a tree, "that Richard greatly resembles his father, the old duke. Was the duke as puny as your son Richard? Was he as short, as pasty-faced, and—deformed?"

"Richard is not deformed!" I exclaimed. "He injured his shoulder at the quintain when he was practicing his jousting. Such injuries are common, as you well know."

The Serpent was silent for a few moments. "So the duke, your husband, was not strong. Perhaps he could not sire healthy sons. Or perhaps it was your fault."

I clenched my hands so tightly together, my nails drew blood.

"Yours was a perfect marriage, except for all those dead children." She paused to pick a red rose. "We Woodvilles take good care of our own. My brother is a good man. Think on it, good mother, I beseech you. For truly I have Richard's best interests at heart!"

She swung around, her green silken skirts making whorls, and left, trailing her brittle laughter.

Chapter 17
Westminster Palace, London
December 1468

Three years and more passed. In July of 1465, Henry of Lancaster was captured and brought to the Tower. In October of 1466, Edward agreed to a treaty of friendship with Philip of Burgundy. From France, the Bitch of Anjou stirred things up by sending Warwick a message. She extended the hand of friendship, deducing correctly the frustration he must now feel.

Matters were not helped, when in July of 1468, Margaret finally married Charles of Burgundy. I did not attend the wedding myself, for it was not the custom to do so for foreign matches. But I listened avidly to the reports of the magnificent ceremony in which the streets of Bruges were hung with priceless tapestries. The parades, feasting, masques and allegorical entertainments so impressed everyone that folk called it *The Wedding of the Century*.

❦

Now it was December of 1468, and I arrived to celebrate Christmas Court with Edward and his Serpent-Queen. I stood by the window, wrapped in a thick fur mantle, my hair in its night plait, gazing at the wintry scene before me. It was so cold the frost had swirled patterns onto the icy windows and the scant vegetation had hardened into ice. What would befall the House of York this season?

I didn't have long to wait, for the door to my chamber burst open, and my nephew Warwick strode in.

"This is insupportable!" he roared.

I bade him sit and signaled to Jenet to bring hot mulled wine and wafers.

But Warwick paced around my chamber, his face flushed darkly, a vein throbbing in his temple.

I waited.

"Cousin," he said finally. "What shall I do about my daughters? There are no eligible heirs to the peerage left for them to marry."

Warwick had no sons, so Bella and Nanette were his heirs, standing to inherit substantial holdings from their Neville, Montacute, and Beauchamp forbears. They were both of an age to marry—Bella, seventeen, and Nanette, twelve.

"You have just come from the Serpent," I stated.

Warwick's mouth crinkled in amusement as I handed him a cup of wine. "You have a gift for nicknames, Aunt."

"What did she say?"

"She had the insolence to suggest that Bella marry her brother Dick, while Nanette should be betrothed to Ned Woodville."

I nodded. "She must be getting desperate to marry off Ned. She once had the temerity to suggest that my Margaret marry him."

He narrowed his eyes. "But Margaret married Burgundy."

My cheeks warmed. I put my hand on his arm. "I know you spent many years working for the alliance with France. But Edward wanted an alliance with Burgundy, and he can be obstinate."

"He was not always that way," said Warwick, his voice rising. "Before he acquired a wife—"

"Before the Serpent came, he was easy to manage. You and I both know that. But now he is different. The Serpent is ensconced in his life, whether we like it or no. Edward will not be ruled by either you or me, so we must devise some other plan."

Warwick glowered. "Those sisters of hers have swept the aristocratic marriage market clean. There is no one suitable left in England. I will not have her loathsome Woodville brothers get their hands on my wealth."

I understood, already alarmed about the marriage prospects for my son George. George was such a handsome boy, tall and blond, the very image of my father. Yet I was having trouble procuring a bride for him. Two years before, Duke Philip of Burgundy had offered his granddaughter's hand in marriage, but Edward would not hear of it. I'd been stunned when George told me the news. In having made a bad marriage, did Edward begrudge a good one for his brother?

At nineteen, George was now the age Edward had been in the first year of his reign. He needed something to do, but the king seemed disinclined to use his brother's talents. George was well educated, I had seen to that. And he showed signs of being a talented administrator, like his father. Yet, if Edward were not going to give George a position in his government, surely he should allow his brother to marry a foreign princess and use his talents abroad?

As if reading my thoughts, Warwick said softly, "It seems the king doesn't want George to marry Mary of Burgundy. So what would you think if George married my Bella?"

I leaned forward, smiling. It was a brilliant idea. "But what of Richard?"

"He can have Nanette."

I mulled this over. I liked it. Warwick's plan did mean giving up any hope of brilliant international marriages for my boys. But with Edward in his present mood, it wasn't likely he would allow Richard to marry a foreign princess, any more than he had allowed George to marry Margaret's stepdaughter. The Neville heiresses were the most suitable young ladies in the whole of England.

"I like it. But we should move cautiously so that Edward doesn't know our full intentions. Richard and Nanette are full young and can wait awhile. I propose that we focus now on getting George wed to Bella. Let me speak with George first."

And so I summoned Jenet to attire me for my appearance at Edward's court and sent a page with a message for George.

"Mother," said George, coming forward to kiss my cheek. "Do you not like my new suit of clothes?" He smiled down at me as I examined him closely. Today he was resplendent in a tunic of purple decorated with intricate gold embroidery. His stockings were of purple and gold with the seam up the middle of each leg. His sleeves were slashed to show the gold shirt he wore under his tunic. His blue-green eyes glowed with excitement. How he loved being at court.

I smiled back at him. "You have such a good eye for color, George," I remarked. "That purple brings out the color of your eyes." I turned around on my stool so that Jenet could pin on my headdress, a pointed henin with a veil of translucent silk.

"Hurry, Mother," he said. "It would not do to be late."

"George." I smiled. "Your mother is an old woman. She is not as fast as she was when she was a girl."

"Nonsense, Mama!" he exclaimed, offering me his arm. "Old? You'll never be old."

I laughed out loud. George always had that effect on me. Though I was fifty-three, George made me feel younger. "I have three grown daughters," I reminded him. "It would not be seemly for their mother to look like a maid."

George threw back his head and roared with laughter. "Now, Mother," he said. "You know you are looking very well."

It was true. Prodded by George, I'd finally decided to abandon my widow's weeds and put on something more cheerful. Today I wore a gown of sky-blue velvet edged in ermine, with silver embroidery running down the sleeves and over my skirts.

Jenet put the last pins into my headdress, and I rose and signaled for her to leave. "I have something important to ask you, my son," I said, leading George to a window seat. "As you know, I think it high time you were married. But I want your opinion on this matter." I paused and looked at him closely. "How would you feel about marrying your cousin Bella?"

At once, his face lit up.

"It would make you happy?"

"Yes, Mother. I am very fond of my cousin. She makes me laugh and—" He flushed. "I've always found her beautiful."

I smiled as I kissed his cheek. "Let's ask cousin Warwick to join us."

❦

Warwick was delighted, and as my nephew and my son conversed, a scene played itself out in my mind, something I had been vaguely thinking of, but had not articulated. When folk grow old, it is the custom for the widowed mother to live with her eldest son in a quiet retirement. But I had been too deeply wounded by Edward's marriage for that to be possible. Suppose I lived with George instead? I adored George; he always made me feel cheerful and energetic. And Bella would be a fine wife for him. Perhaps I could live out my life in the company of George and his family.

George offered me his arm, and we left for the formal banquet that Edward was giving as part of the Christmas celebrations at court. These celebrations were very elaborate, both in terms of the number of courses served, as well as the strict protocol the Serpent insisted on. I was very glad to have my handsome son beside me, radiating energy and good cheer, for I found these occasions wearisome in the extreme.

"Now remember," I said in a low voice, "today is the feast of Christ's birth, of peace and joy upon the land. We must put on a good appearance of one happy family. You understand, my son?"

George's expression darkened.

"You will be polite to the queen." I was careful not to call her by her nickname in front of George, because he was acquiring a disturbing tendency to blurt out secrets. But now I was going to take George firmly in hand. First, it was imperative that he learn some skills to arm himself against the Serpent's poison.

"What would you have me do?" said George, his lower lip jutting out sulkily.

"The only way to deal with her is to be polite and ignore everything she says. She will attempt to bait you, to goad you into saying things you should not say. Remember it gives her the greatest pleasure to upset us. You must, however, remain silent or turn the conversation. Try not to listen to her, and whatever you do, you must not rise to her bait. She is adept at spotting her opponent's weaknesses."

George nodded and I took his arm again. I resolved to stay as close to him as I could without being too obvious about it.

The Serpent was ensconced by the fire, clad in a magnificent dress of silver and blood-red brocade. In four and a half years of marriage, she'd given Edward two children, both daughters, and now she was heavily pregnant with their third child. Edward sat next to her, and of course her numerous Woodville relatives surrounded them: her father and mother, her six brothers, and her nine sisters with their stolen husbands.

I was forced to sit by the windows, facing them, with Warwick and his family on one side, and George on the other. Icy fingers of air made their way through the casements, chilling my fingers. I placed them in the folds of my new velvet gown.

A flurry of movement caught my eye. One of the Serpent's sisters, Jacqueline, had wandered over a few feet away and started nibbling at some nuts. She looked like a rabbit with her fine, strong teeth, and as she talked, she continued to nibble.

"How fare you, sweet Johnny?" she said to her brother. Sir John Woodville was a well-made young man of three-and-twenty years.

"I fare well," he replied evenly.

"How does marriage suit you?" Nibble, nibble.

"She is very kind."

"She does not excite your passion then?" Nibble, nibble.

John sighed but made no reply.

"Is she not too old for you?" Nibble.

John occupied himself in taking his new kid gloves off. They were dyed black to match his hose and fit perfectly to his shapely hands.

"How have you the patience to bear it? Why, she has no teeth, her breath is foul, and she—"

John shushed his sister with a wave of his hand.

I turned. Cath stood in the doorway. Her eyes moved slowly around the room, and as they lighted on her husband John, she smiled. She went over to kiss him full on the lips.

"I found the tincture I told you about, the one for sore throats and colds. Come with me, my darling."

During this speech, John made various gestures, intended to slow the volume and rapidity of Cath's speech. At seventy-one, she was deaf and difficult to understand, having lost most of her teeth. She stood there, looking at her husband lovingly, drooling; when suddenly noticing this, she fumbled for a kerchief, flushed, and excused herself.

Poor Cath; my heart ached. I glanced at my son Edward. He was talking to my Richard, clapping him on the back and laughing merrily. And Richard's face showed an unusual amount of animation.

I made myself sit ramrod straight in my seat, gritting my teeth to forestall the impending headache always produced by the Serpent's presence. But Jacqueline had not the good manners to hide the look of disgust on her face. "Couldn't you get this marriage annulled?"

Her bell-like voice rang out as silence suddenly filled the room. My gorge rose. I stood.

"Don't you think you should keep your wicked thoughts to yourself?" I snapped. The nibbling stopped.

The Serpent, her face impassive, rose and faced me. Casually stifling a yawn, she lumbered slowly towards George and held out her hand. "Come, brother. Come, keep me company. You know how to play piquet, no?"

George flushed as he rose and bowed to her. They went to sit near the fireplace with her family.

I went slowly back towards my place near the window, taking care to take a seat that was in earshot of the proceedings.

"You're a good-looking boy, you should be married," the Serpent said.

Nineteen-year-old George smiled but refrained from saying anything.

The Serpent deftly cut the cards and shuffled. "I have a little sister."

"Another sister?" blurted out George. "I thought your sisters to be all married."

"All except for one. My sister Agnes would do very well for you."

I should have been prepared for this, but I was not. Was there no end to the Serpent's coils? I drew my handkerchief from my sleeve, and dried my moist palms.

"How old is the lady?"

"She turned twelve last month. She's a sweet child, and well suited to you." The Serpent stared at George, as she dealt the cards. "She pouts, and sulks, and is easily led." She paused, and smiled. "She would be the perfect playmate for your little games."

George sat stone still, a flush spreading slowly up his neck, staring at the card-strewn table before him. Suddenly, he leapt up, knocking over his chair. "How dare you insult me like this!" George jutted out his lower lip, making him look exactly like a sulky child.

The Serpent smiled sweetly.

I put my finger to my lips, but George ignored me.

"I already have a bride," he said.

The Serpent's cat's eyes went wide.

"Sweeting!" she called across the room to Edward. "Were you aware that your dear brother planned to marry?"

Edward rose, his blue eyes blazing. "Who is she?"

George faced him, scowling. "You don't have any right—"

"Who is she?"

George flicked a look over at me.

I nodded.

"Cousin Bella."

"What?" roared Edward.

"Why not?"

Edward shushed him with a wave of his hand. "I expressly forbid you," he said loudly into the dead silence that followed, "to marry your cousin Bella."

"It's not right!" exclaimed George. "You block me at every turn. You prevented my marriage to Mary of Burgundy. Now you won't let me marry Bella. Just because you've married a whore yourself doesn't mean you can prevent me from making a good match."

Edward went white. "You will apologize," he said in a voice that cut like a knife.

George glared at him as Warwick went to stand by his side.

Edward put his hand on the Serpent's shoulder. "You are talking of my wife, your liege lady, and my Queen."

The Serpent covered his hand with her own and turned to smile up at him. They were a fortress together against the rest of the world. How had I failed in my attempts to pry Edward away from the Serpent?

My belly filling with ice, slowly, I stood.

Gradually, everyone in the room turned to stare at me.

"I am displeased with you, my son," I said. My voice rang like a bell in the thick silence. "You have grievously offended your family, your cousin Warwick, your brothers George and Richard, and your mother. I am deeply hurt by what you have done. All my life, I have supported and cherished you, yet how do you repay me?" I paused and jabbed my finger at the Serpent: "By marrying someone who is not worthy."

Edward flushed and took a step towards me. He said loudly, "She *is* worthy, Mother."

I lifted my chin and stared him down. "She is a canker in the House of York. She is destroying it even as we speak."

Edward narrowed his eyes and went pale. The silence was deafening.

"I am disappointed. I thought you once worthy to be my lord husband's heir. Instead, I see you betray your father's low origins."

There was a swelling murmur as folk turned to each other and whispered.

"My father was the Duke of York."

"*Your* father," said I, my voice tinkling like ice, "was an archer on the Rouen garrison. His name was Blaybourne. His father, your grandsire, was not even a knight, but a humble blacksmith—"

"You lie!" roared Edward, coming towards me.

"I do not," I replied. I turned to face everyone in the room. "I am willing to go before a public enquiry to answer any questions, even to swear an oath on Holy Writ or saint's bones or a vial of the most precious blood of Our Lord and Savior Jesus Christ, that what I say is most true. This man," I indicated Edward, "Is a bastard. He is a fraud and an impostor, and I have made him so, for I loved and dedicated my life to him."

My voice broke. How I had loved Blaybourne. How I had allowed Edward's likeness to my lover to blind me to his faults.

"I see now how wrong I was. For you cannot make a noble out of dross. He is my child, yes, but no blood relation to the Duke of York, my late husband."

My voice rose at the end of this speech. I felt someone beside me. It was Richard.

"Mother!" he exclaimed, his blue-grey eyes cloudy with distress.

Was he worried about his own paternity? I would set the record straight.

"The true heir to the throne of England is my son George, followed in succession by his younger brother Richard. They are my lord husband's legitimate heirs."

My voice rang eerily through that packed chamber. I paused for a moment, then allowed Richard to lead me to my rooms.

The last thing I remember just before the door shut was a tableau of Edward, white and shaking on one side of the room, and George, standing proud and tall on the other side of the room, his blue-green eyes blazing with excitement.

Chapter 18
December 1468 to March 1469

Within the hour, I left for Fotheringhay. It was time for me to retire and lead a life of quiet contemplation.

They came for me in March.

I was standing in the collegiate church of Fotheringhay, talking to the glazier who had just finished beautifying the windows at my direction.

"We come from the king!" someone shouted.

I ignored this individual, for I was not accustomed to being greeted in such a rough manner.

My steward appeared, breathless from running. "They say they are from the king, madam." He bowed.

I turned and fixed the churls with an icy stare. There were ten of them, dressed simply, in leather jerkins and nondescript woolen clothing. They carried quarter-staves and sported daggers in their belts. They looked like the sort of rude men-of-arms one would use to garrison a castle, not deal with a great lady. The person with the loud voice took a scroll out of his leather bag, unrolled it, and declaimed as follows:

> *From Edward, King of England, to Cecylee, Duchess of York, Greetings.*
>
> *I, Edward, King of England, do arrest you, Cecylee Duchess of York, on the charge of treason for bruiting abroad scurrilous rumors about my person. I command you, therefore, to follow these men to Berkhamsted, where I shall confine you under armed guard for the rest of your life.*

I frowned. Before I could make sense of this, one of the churls grabbed my arm. "It is time to go, my fine lady."

I shook him off.

"We have orders to escort you to Berkhamsted."

"Impossible. I cannot go now. And be so good as to take your filthy paw off my arm."

The men guffawed. "I see you are not called Proud Cis for nothing," one of them remarked.

"Proud Cis! Proud Cis! Proud Cis!" chanted the others.

A cold wind blew, and my flesh hardened into ice. If these men truly were from Edward, it meant there was nothing he might not do to insult and humiliate me.

"I demand to see the warrant," I said, my voice high.

The men laughed again. "Quite a mouse we have here," remarked one wit.

My steward stood in front of them. "You are insulting the king's mother."

The loud-mouthed man curled his lip. "If she tears it up and burns it, let her know that I have other copies, signed and sealed by the king's hand."

I took the warrant from my steward and scanned it. It was signed by Edward, I recognized his writing and his seal.

I crumpled onto a stone seat. "What about my household?"

"The king, your son, declares that you will do without a household. You are to leave forthwith. He will brook no delay."

❦

I left Fotheringhay, the home that Richard and I had made together for over twenty years, to the sounds of my household weeping. They did at least allow me to ride my best palfrey and to wrap myself up in furs to keep out the cold. But the weather was bitter with icy winds by day and frosts by night. As I rode the eighty miles to Berkhamsted in Hertfordshire, I wondered if I would die from cold, damp, sorrow, and humiliation. Bitterly did I regret my words. Far from abandoning Edward, the Serpent had drawn even closer and connived to send me to Berkhamsted in disgrace.

At length, we arrived. My head reverberated with the sound of the Serpent's brittle laughter as I looked around. The towers leaned and the roof over the great hall had fallen in. My rough escorts left me in the muddy courtyard, sitting bedraggled on my coffer. It was sleeting hard. They took my horse away and drew straws to determine who would guard me while the others foraged.

The dull afternoon was darkening slowly when, through lines of sleet, a black shape came into view. I stiffened. Was this figure Death? Had my lord Richard come for me? Or was it one of the men, determined to humiliate me further?

"My lady," said the figure in a high voice, "my name is Ghislaine." She curtseyed low, muddying her skirts as she did so.

I beckoned and the figure let down her hood. She was a finely made girl of around twelve or so with delicate pale features and grey eyes.

"Child, what are you doing here?"

"My parents are gone, so I must find my own keep," she replied. "The sisters at the convent of Ashridge took me on as a maid. They asked me to walk over here, to see if you needed anything."

I took breath. Ghislaine's pale face surrounded by wisps of hair beaded with moisture, and her patched clothes stirred a memory. Hadn't Blaybourne said that he was turned out of his home at the age of seven, no one willing to look after him?

I sat upright on my seat and patted the girl's head. "We must get out of this sleet, child, or we shall both catch our death." I looked over at the guard who had been left to watch me: "You, sir. What is your name?"

To my astonishment, he bowed. "Gerard, my lady, at your service." After the rough treatment this past week, I had not thought anyone would be polite to me again. Gerard was a short, compact gentleman, of around five and twenty, with a spade-shaped beard and square hands.

"Master Gerard," said I, rising. "If you would be so good as to follow me with the cart, I will show you where to put everything." I turned to Ghislaine. "Do you know how to make a fire?"

"Yes, my lady," she replied curtseying again. "And I can cook and sew."

"That is well enough for now, child. Let us get out of this evil weather."

There was but one room fit for habitation, and that was the solar. It was a large room, big enough for my furniture. But to get to it one was obliged to walk up a rickety staircase open to the elements, then heave open a door that was hanging off its hinges. Somehow, Master Gerard hoisted all of my possessions up those stairs without dropping anything and arranged the furniture at my direction.

I had my bed put against the inner wall and the carved chairs set on each side of the fireplace. I directed Gerard to put the hangings up to ward off the damp chill that pervaded the place.

Clearly, the Serpent hoped I would make a quick end of it here.

I resolved to disappoint her.

I told Ghislaine to make the fire, put the water on to boil, and arrange my down bedspreads, cushions, pillows, and gleaming gold cups while I unpacked my dresses from the coffer.

The door banged to and fro on its weakened hinge, letting in flurries of snow, as well as drafts of cold air.

"Good day to you, madam," said a voice.

I turned. A young woman in a Benedictine habit was curtseying.

"Though it be so dark, you can scarce tell it be day," she remarked. "I am Sister Avisa, of the Benedictine Order of Nuns at the convent of Ashridge, beyond the hamlet of Friesden, not four miles hence. We have come to make you welcome."

She waved in a young man, who bore the royal arms of the leopards of Anjou and the lilies of France.

He knelt and handed up a letter from Edward, which announced the birth of his third daughter. The child was to be named Cecily in my honor.

I looked up to scrutinize the countenance of the messenger before me. But his expression revealed nothing.

I walked to the window to collect my thoughts. It was sleeting hard again, and everything dissolved into grey shadows as afternoon waned into evening. What was the meaning of this? The last time I'd seen Edward was just after I told everyone he was illegitimate. He'd been furious, and when he was furious, he could be terrifying. Since that day, he'd sent no message to me. The only communication had been that arrest warrant.

I read the letter again slowly. In Edward's fine Italic hand, it told me I would be allowed to return to court, provided I made a public apology to the King and the Serpent and retracted my words.

Tears filled my eyes. I brushed them away and turned to Sister Avisa.

"I am greatly fatigued," I told her. "Would you see to it that a suitable gift is sent for the child, and please tell my son I am retiring from the world?"

"Do you wish me to add anything else?"

"Tell him that I am retiring to my new home in the country that he was gracious enough to give me."

Sister Avisa curtseyed silently and left.

I sank into my chair and covered my face with my hands.

I would not know Edward's children well. I saw the two so-called Little Princes in the Tower—Edward of Westminster and his brother, Richard of Shrewsbury, the Duke of York—fewer times than I could count with the fingers of one hand.

❦

A week later, my steward from Fotheringhay, my maid Jenet, and others of my household arrived with more of my things.

"But what will the King say?" I asked, as my people from Fotheringhay bowed and curtseyed before me. "He'll not allow you to stay."

"He'll not cause me to go," declared Jenet. "I was worried sick about you. You know how susceptible you are to the cold, and the weather has been evil. Look at the way you're coughing, even now. 'My place is with my lady,' I said to myself. For no one else can make the cold tinctures that she needs."

"And I am right glad to see you," I replied, kissing her on the cheek. "And all of you are welcome," I added, "if you wish to stay in this grim place."

They assured me that they wished to stay with such a kind mistress and set about making needful repairs.

Slowly, life returned to normal.

Unfortunately, the same could not be said for my nearest kin. Things had curdled to sourness betwixt my son and my nephew. Warwick had given up much of his life, as well as a portion of his considerable fortune, to support the House of York. And what had Edward done for him in return? Promoted the Serpent's family at the expense of everyone else.

Now he made difficulties about the marriage between George and Bella. Edward's opposition did not prevent Warwick from working behind the scenes to obtain a papal dispensation so that the marriage could proceed.

I gazed out at the gloomy skies that seemed to hover over this ruined castle. What would Edward do when George defied him and married Bella?

Chapter 19
June 1469 to September 1470

In June of 1469, three months after I was taken from my home in Fotheringhay, news came that George plotted to overthrow Edward.

I motioned the messenger to leave and went to my *prie-dieu* for prayer and reflection. Wasn't this what I wanted? But what about George? Would he have the backing of the magnates and the citizens of London? Or was this a ploy by Warwick to seize power?

I let the polished jet beads of my rosary slip through my fingers. George was in great danger, I was sure of it. As his mother, I must do everything in my power to protect him.

And so I hurried to Canterbury, where he was then staying, awaiting a favorable tide that would take him to Calais.

"My son," I said. "Do not do this. It will ruin your life."

"Edward is a bastard. You said so, yourself. Mother, I am the legitimate heir to the throne."

"I know, my son. But I know also that Edward has been anointed king, and that he is popular with the people."

"Warwick is more popular."

George had a point there. The people were growing weary of the taxes Edward imposed on them, and there was unrest in the north.

I took a deep breath, then played my last card. "Warwick does not want you on the throne."

George's eyes narrowed. For a moment, he looked exactly like Edward. "How do you know that?"

"I feel it in my bones."

"Then why is he supporting me?"

"He is using you."

George turned away. "Go home, Mother, and leave me in peace. I have pledged my word to Warwick's cause, and I'll not go back on it."

I argued with him for an hour or more, but there was nothing I could do to sway his judgment.

And so I returned to Berkhamsted.

At the beginning of July, George set sail for Calais with Warwick and his family. Shortly afterwards, the unrest in the north boiled over. Edward did nothing. Instead he took a boat to Fotheringhay and spent a week in my newly refurbished apartments. With the Serpent.

On the eleventh day of July 1469, in defiance of Edward's wishes, George wed Warwick's daughter Bella in the Church of Our Lady in Calais. Then, Warwick issued a proclamation calling on the king to remove the Woodvilles from their high offices. Warwick sailed for Kent, marched on the city of London, where he was welcomed with great acclaim, then went north.

On the twenty-sixth day of July 1469, Warwick scored a resounding victory at the Battle of Edgecote Moor.

Edward, who had been woolgathering in the middle of the country, now sought shelter in a little village called Olney. When news of Warwick's victory broke, all the lords left him, saving only his distant cousin William Hastings, whose father had long served the House of York, and my youngest son, Richard, Duke of Gloucester.

On the second day of August 1469, Edward was captured and brought before Warwick and George.

On hearing this news, I fainted.

When I came to, I went to my *prie-dieu* and spent the rest of the day on my knees in prayer. For if Edward were now to be executed, I would be responsible. Little did I think that my bitter words would be used against him so quickly, and to such lethal effect.

The next morning, I sent a messenger to invite the nuns from house of Ashridge to join me at Berkhamsted Castle. Thus, I gradually fell into the habit of rising early to pray at matins, of having religious works read aloud while I dined, and of relaxing in the evening with my women over a glass or two of wine. The daily rhythm of prayer as well as the company of the good sisters helped me to keep my sanity.

For the news sent me spinning, like a top.

The Serpent got exactly what she deserved, forced to lodge in the Tower in scant state. Now she would know how it felt to come down in the world. Her mother's arrest on a charge of witchcraft was only to be expected since it was well known she practiced the black arts. That is exactly how she trapped my son into that awful marriage. The capture and beheading of the Serpent's father and one of her brothers was regrettable. But how else was one to get rid of the Woodvilles? They were everywhere, a blight on the White Rose of York.

Then I received a tear-stained letter from Cath in which she bewailed the passing of her fourth husband, Sir John Woodville:

> *My Johnny was so sweet,* wrote Cath, *and such a good husband to me. I cannot imagine what he did to deserve such a death. I hope, dear sister, your dislike of the Queen did not cause you to say things you might regret. You always were headstrong, you know.*

I crumpled up the letter and tossed it in the fire. Then I took to my bed, Jenet fussing over me with her tonics and tinctures.

Yes, the Serpent had gone. But what about my sons? What was going to happen to Edward, George, Richard?

Despite his popularity, Warwick did not have the authority to rule. Without the support of the magnates, ruling England would prove impossible, and the majority of the magnates thought that this time Warwick had gone too far. By summer's end, Warwick was losing his grip and the country was descending into anarchy. In London, angry mobs demanded the release of the king.

Edward was released from captivity and taken to York where his supporters and the magnates acclaimed him.

Early in October of 1469, Edward left York with his supporters and returned to London to the great joy of its citizens. One of his first acts was to give Richard, then only seventeen years old, full powers to secure the Welsh strongholds from rebel hands.

I smiled when I read a letter from my youngest son, in which he earnestly told me how he had successfully carried out the king's instructions. I locked the letter away in a box I kept by my bed to read when my spirits became low.

Although Edward behaved courteously towards George and Warwick, it was plain to all that things were not going their way. By February of 1470, Warwick's desperation with the situation had reached such a pitch, he incited a rising in Yorkshire and Lincolnshire. His plan was to distract Edward in this manner, then enlist the help of the French king in deposing him.

This time, Edward acted quickly and marched north. The king's army confronted the rebels at Empingham in Rutland on the twelfth day of March 1470, and it struck so swiftly that Warwick and George had no time to bring in reinforcements. The rebels fled with such speed they left their jackets behind. And so this battle became known as the Battle of Lose-Coat Field.

On the twenty-fourth of March 1470, Edward issued a proclamation calling Warwick and George traitors and rebels. They fled to Calais, taking Warwick's wife, George's wife, and Bella's younger sister, Nanette.

Then tragedy struck.

On the sixteenth day of April 1470, Bella, heavily pregnant, went into labor.

> *Our first child could not be saved,* wrote George in a letter to me, *for we were all on a ship at anchor in Calais Harbor, and Edward's henchmen would not let us land in Calais. When Cousin Warwick pleaded with them, saying that his daughter was like to die, they replied that they had received direct orders from King Edward himself. Can you believe it? I had not thought him to be cruel. Bella lost a lot of blood. She owes her life to her mother, cousin Anne, who is skilled in midwifery.*

I shook my head. The continuation of the war was making men bitter. Even Edward, usually so genial and tolerant, forgot his knightly code. Taking George's letter, I went to my *prie-dieu* and placed it between my hands. I spent an hour or so praying to God that George and Bella would have healthy children.

Things continued to go badly for George. Warwick gained an audience with the King of France and was persuaded to make reconciliation with Marguerite of Anjou, then staying at the French court with her son, Édouard. As I had foreseen, George was set aside. For King Louis XI thought it better to try and reinstate Henry of Lancaster, rather than put George on the throne, telling Warwick that George was unreliable.

It did not take George long to realize what was afoot, and the letter he wrote me was an angry one. I resisted telling him off. Instead, I wrote a soothing note in which I expressed the hope that he might reconcile himself to Edward, f*or he is your sovereign lord*, I wrote, *and greatly beloved by the people.*

I wondered how Louis XI had persuaded Marguerite d'Anjou to make peace with Warwick. I had an opportunity to find out when the French ambassador traveled up from London to pay his respects.

"It was not easy, madam," he replied, smiling faintly in reply to my question. "Queen Marguerite cried out that Warwick had pierced her heart with wounds that would bleed until Judgment Day, when she would appeal to the justice of God for vengeance against him."

"Not an auspicious beginning," I remarked, signaling for more wine to be poured.

Now that I had been at Berkhamsted for over a year, the place was beginning to look like a royal palace again, where I might entertain visitors without embarrassment. Edward had graciously forgotten to take my revenues away from me, so I was able to pay for the upkeep and refurbishment of this place, which had been home to so many English queens.

"It was not an auspicious beginning," agreed the ambassador, wiping his lips with a napkin. "But King Louis is very patient. He heard her out and, when she finished, told her bluntly that while her arguments might be valid, she should put her personal feelings aside if she wished to win the throne back for her husband."

"And she agreed to this?"

"Only after a discussion that lasted many, many days."

On the fifteenth of July 1470, Warwick's wife, Anne, and his daughter Nanette were formally presented to Marguerite d'Anjou. Ten days later, on July 25, Nanette was betrothed to Marguerite's son Édouard in Angers Cathedral. Five days later, on July 30, Warwick swore to keep faith with the Lancastrians on a fragment of the true cross.

In August, Edward, who had ignored the warnings from his diplomats and went hunting, was drawn north to Yorkshire by news of a rebellion.

On the thirteenth of September, Warwick's fleet of ships arrived in the West Country harbors of Dartmouth and Plymouth. So many men flocked to Warwick's banner, by the time he reached Coventry, he had an army numbering some fifty thousand men.

Edward marched south to deal with Warwick's rebellion only to find his soldiers deserting in large numbers. And so he fled to Burgundy, taking with him his boon companion William Hastings, his brother-in-law Rivers, and my youngest son Richard.

Chapter 20
October 1470 to October 1471

My three sons now fought over the throne of England. It was impossible for me to take sides; however much I disagreed with Edward over his choice of wife, he had been a good king. Moreover, Richard, of whom I was so proud, adored his brother the king. He had followed him into exile, even though it meant fighting against his former mentor and friend, Warwick. As for George, I could never now think of him without the greatest anxiety. What was to become of him? His life seemed rudderless and dark.

We rode into London at the head of a triumphal procession, wrote George, *and made homage to King Henry. Cousin Warwick ordered the king to be newly arrayed in a robe of blue velvet, and we rode from the Tower along Cheapside to the Bishop of London's palace. Warwick had him sit on the throne and placed the crown on his head. He paid him great reverence. But I could not help noticing that King Henry sat on the throne as if he were but a sack of wool. Was he always like that, Mother? For you knew him well in his younger days.*

I smiled grimly as I tucked that letter away. The fact the King Henry seemed so inert caused a small spark of hope to light in my heart. But where were Edward and Richard?

Soon after, I received a letter from Richard.

Madam,

I recommend me to you as heartily as is to me possible. Edward and I and others of our party have arrived in The Hague, so you need fret no more, Mother. We are safe. We are going to seek out Charles of Burgundy, and in my next, I hope to bring you tidings of our sister Margaret.

On the second day of November 1470, the Serpent gave birth to a son, named Edward. It should have been a day of great rejoicing, for after three daughters, she had given Edward his heir. But the Serpent was perching in Westminster

Abbey where she had taken sanctuary. And Warwick reigned supreme.

However, the birth of the Yorkist heir disquieted Warwick. On the thirteenth of December 1470, his fourteen-year-old daughter Nanette was married to seventeen-year-old Édouard of Lancaster, now styled Prince of Wales, in the Château d'Amboise. Marguerite of Anjou was in attendance.

Then, Warwick blundered.

I received this news one cold, wet morning in February of 1471 when a messenger ran into the great hall of Berkhamsted Castle.

"He's ordered the Calais garrison to attack Burgundy!"

I straightened in my seat on the dais, and frowned. "What mean you, my good fellow?"

The messenger gasped out something that I could not clearly hear.

I signaled to my steward. "Bring a pitcher of ale and some pies from the kitchens."

As he hurried off to do my bidding, I recognized the messenger as being one of my late husband's agents. I beckoned him closer.

"Tell me your message more slowly, my good friend. Of whom are you speaking?"

"Warwick, my lady. Warwick has ordered the Calais garrison to attack Burgundy."

"Are you sure?" I said, watching his face closely.

The messenger gazed squarely into my eyes, his expression never changing.

I frowned as I settled more comfortably against the cushions in my carved chair: "That seems extremely foolhardy. If he did that, there would be no better way of throwing Charles of Burgundy into Edward's arms."

"Indeed, madam. Which is why I am here. To bring you good comfort."

I smiled. Edward and Richard would have an opportunity to invade England after all. But their path would be fraught with danger.

"Tell me about the London merchants," I said, motioning him to rise. "Do they know of this matter?"

"Indeed they do, and they are furious. The do not want England dragged into a war with Burgundy without Parliament's consent. They know this could ruin their trade. And so, they are refusing to lend Warwick any more money."

The tide is turning, I thought, giving the messenger a sovereign.

On the fourteenth of March 1471, Edward landed in Ravenspur, Yorkshire with an army funded by the Duke of Burgundy. Four days later on March 18, he was welcomed into the city of York. On the twenty-ninth of March, Edward appeared before Coventry, one of the most heavily fortified towns in England, for his spies had told him that Warwick was there with seven thousand men.

Edward spent three days sending formal challenges to Warwick to come out and fight, to no avail. Edward then marched his army to Warwick and captured the castle. There, he was formally proclaimed king.

I took this opportunity to write to George:

My beloved son,

You can see how little you stand with Warwick, for I am told that he recently forced you to hand over some of your property to Marguerite d'Anjou. I pray you, therefore, to put aside your differences and give Edward your assistance in regaining his throne. Edward is generous with his rewards, and your elderly mother will rejoice to see her sons reunited.

On the third of April, George, Duke of Clarence, led his army of twelve thousand men into King Edward's camp at Banbury and knelt in submission. On the eleventh of April, another messenger ran into Berkhamsted Castle.

"The king has arrived in London!" he exclaimed.

I rose from my seat, flooded with energy. "Heavens be praised. How was he greeted?"

"With great joy, madam," replied the messenger bowing. He handed me a letter with a flourish. "He had with him his brothers of Clarence and Gloucester."

"Thanks be to God," I exclaimed, crossing myself.

Edward's letter invited me to meet him in London. And so, it came to pass, that Edward, George, and Richard attended a solemn service in my private chapel on April 12, 1471, Good Friday.

As I walked down the stairs into the great hall of Baynard's Castle to greet my three sons, I finally felt some measure of peace. How wonderful that they were together at last. For this was the way it was supposed to be, brother supporting brother.

To celebrate the occasion, I invited several leading citizens of London and their wives. It was heart-warming to hear so many kind folk inquire after my health and express their delight that I was back in London. I was in the middle of talking with Sir Simon Eyre, former sheriff and mayor of London, who was telling me his memories of my lord Richard, when twenty-eight-year -old Edward strode boisterously into the hall, looking fit and lean after his exertions in the field. As was his wont, he had no trouble filling that huge room with his presence.

"Mother!" he bellowed, kissing me on both cheeks. "How good it is to see you again."

I had no time to register any emotion, for he immediately turned away, and began shaking hands, clapping people on the back, and patting arms, laughing boisterously all the while as the Londoners crowded around him.

He was followed by Richard, now eighteen years old, but looking ten years older. As usual, Richard seemed content to remain in Edward's shadow, looking watchful and grave, while Edward charmed everyone.

I took Richard's hands in greeting as he kissed me on both cheeks. He would never be indolent like Edward, but would he be as well liked? He was too difficult to read.

Last to arrive was George, making an awkward third spoke of a wheel. He pecked me on the cheek, then circled the room studying his brothers, running his tongue over his lips.

What was going to happen to George? Would he ever keep his word again? Or had he been corrupted beyond redemption by Warwick?

Edward held a great counsel at Baynard's Castle, then marched north to deal with Warwick. On Easter Sunday, at dawn, near the village of Barnet, Edward fell upon Warwick's army and soundly defeated him. Warwick was cut down fleeing from the scene. When Marguerite d' Anjou, newly arrived in England, heard the news, she collapsed into a faint. Her commanders persuaded her to stay and fight.

This time, Edward wasted no time in marching out of London to the West Country to intercept Marguerite and Édouard to prevent them from crossing the Severn into Wales.

On the fourth of May 1470, they met at Tewkesbury, near Gloucester. With the help of my youngest son, Richard, Duke of Gloucester, Edward won the day. And Marguerite's son Édouard was cut down.

I closed my ears to tales that Édouard survived the fighting and was murdered after the battle in cold blood by my three sons. I tried not to hear the whispers that Henry of Lancaster, the former King Henry VI, was struck down while at prayer. Some said that Richard of Gloucester was responsible for his murder. That he had come up silently behind King Henry before cracking his head open with a mace.

I turned a deaf ear to these rumors because I was grateful that the Cousin's War was over. Nearly ten years after my lord's murder, the House of York had prevailed.

On the twenty-first of May 1470, Edward was formally welcomed into London by the populace. In his train was Marguerite of Anjou, enduring the taunts of the crowd as they threw rubbish at her. Meanwhile, on the twenty-second of May 1470, Henry of Lancaster's corpse was taken to Saint Paul's so that all might pay their respects. The people of London were saddened by Henry of Lancaster's passing, but thankful to be rid of their weak king. Marguerite was imprisoned in the Tower of London. But Edward, in a merciful gesture, sent her to live in Wallingford Castle so she could be near her great friend Alice Chaucer, the Dowager Duchess of Suffolk.

Dearest Mother, wrote Beth, *you may have heard that the former queen has come to live nearby, owing to her friendship with my mother-by-marriage, Duchess Alice. Edward wrote to me, asking me to accompany the Dowager Duchess as much as possible on her visits to the former queen. I assured him I would do my best, for you know I am good at keeping quiet.*

I laughed. George's nickname for Beth had been *Mouse*, she had been such a quiet child in contrast to her noisy siblings. I picked up the letter.

I take my basket of sewing things and sit in a corner making clothes for my children, doing the fine needlework you taught us, Mother, while the ladies talk. So far, I have nothing interesting to report to the king, for while Marguerite bewails her state, the duchess comforts her with gifts and wise sayings. She has made sure that the former queen is comfortably appointed at Wallingford Castle, with three women to serve her. I will write more when I have news. I pray for you every night, dear Mother.

Your loving, Beth, Duchess of Suffolk.

I sighed, tucking the letter away. At least one of my daughters was nearby and dutiful. Margaret wrote wonderful letters, but I never saw her now that she was Duchess of Burgundy. I scarcely saw Nan, and when I did, it was like speaking to a stranger. And though things were somewhat mended between Edward and myself, they were not the same. I was ashamed that George must stomach a bastard half-brother on the throne of England. If only I had said no that far-off evening thirty years ago.

But one cannot undo the past.

Chapter 21
October 1471

I was most proud of my youngest son, Richard, Duke of Gloucester, whose motto was *Loyauté Me Lié* (*Loyalty Binds Me*). Richard was the hero of the Battle of Barnet, holding the line against overwhelming odds, so that Edward did not need to send in his reserves until the last moment. The king could be very generous, and Richard had been heaped with honors for his role in the Yorkist victory. After the Battle of Tewkesbury, I orchestrated a campaign whereby my daughters pleaded for clemency, on George's behalf, which Edward eventually granted. But he refused to give George anything. This led to an outbreak of feuding between my two younger sons, and it erupted at around the time when my quiet, hard to read Richard decided to marry.

Richard and I had been the best of friends ever since the Serpent tried to take him from Warwick and send him to her brother Sir Anthony Woodville. On that evening long ago, I invited Richard to dine with me to ascertain his wishes. Not surprisingly, he preferred to stay with Warwick. As he left, I made a casual remark: "My son, I wish for you to find happiness in this life."

He looked at me, puzzled, his grave expression making him look much older than twelve years.

I touched his cheek with my finger. "When I was a girl, I danced and sang and played music all day long. I think of my childhood as a golden time. I was always misbehaving, but you, my son, have not had that. The war took your childhood from you. I wish I could lighten your cares. You are too young to be so serious. But then, you are just like your father."

Richard's face came alive. "Am I really?"

I nodded. "You look exactly like him. You have his nut-brown hair, his blue-grey eyes, his small build. And you have his serious personality."

"Is this true, Mother?"

"Richard! You didn't think—"

"No, Mother," he replied, flushing. He fiddled with a ring Edward had given him. "I don't look like Edward or George—"

That was true. Both Edward and George were blond giants.

"That is because Edward and George both take after my father, especially George," I told him. That was not quite true. Edward looked exactly like Blaybourne, but I didn't tell Richard that. "Meanwhile you look like your father. How odd you both share the same name."

"Tell me about my father," he said eagerly.

And so, over the months and years that passed, I gradually told Richard about my lord of York, and from that day forward, we became the best of friends.

I suppose my guilty feelings caused me to overdo the image I gave Richard of his father. In his eyes, Richard of York became a hero, a shining warrior, an upholder of knightly virtues, the perfect gentleman. What harm could there be in it? It gave my romantic youngest son something to reach for, something to measure his conduct by. Such a different standard from the frivolity and debauchery of Edward's court.

And now, nineteen-year-old Richard had come to visit me at Berkhamsted. As always, I was delighted to see him. As was our custom, we went into my private chapel to pray for a while before sitting down to talk. This time, Richard was not as quiet as usual. He kept pacing back and forth, fiddling with the signet ring.

I ordered refreshments, then waved my people away.

"What is it?" I poured the mulled wine, for the October days were chill, and Richard had ridden at breakneck speed from London by the look of his boots.

"I wish to marry, Mother," said Richard, tossing his gloves onto a nearby coffer. "I wish to marry Nanette."

My head jerked up. Richard had just been preoccupied in fighting for the Yorkist cause. Where had he found the time to think of taking a wife?

"But Nanette is recently widowed," I said. Not long after her father Warwick had married her off to Édouard of Lancaster, he'd been killed at the Battle of Tewkesbury. "What about a foreign princess? There is Mary of Burgundy, who has now fourteen years."

"I want Nanette." Richard's tone was quiet but firm, his grey-blue eyes dark with intensity.

I recognized that look. It was the exact same expression my lord had had when he'd asked me to marry him all those years ago.

Sighing, I motioned him to sit beside me. "Nanette is lovely, and perfectly suitable. Yet—"

"What, Mother?"

"She is—delicate. I am not sure she will be able to give you children. Even trying to have one child may be too much for her."

Richard paled, and his face went still. He was silent.

At last, I gently touched his arm. "Richard, my son, I am deeply sorry if I have wounded you. I did not know how much you cared about her."

"I have loved her from the moment I set eyes on her."

"But you were only eight! She was four."

"She was an angel," murmured Richard.

"Why did you not say so before? My son, you carry too many burdens. I had no idea. How you must have suffered when you heard—"

"She'd been married to that brute Lancaster?" Richard smiled wryly. "Part of me died, but it inspired me to fight."

"And you fought brilliantly, my son. I'm so proud of you."

Richard smiled. "So you will help me, Mother?"

I laughed. "Why do you need my help?"

"She's disappeared."

"Disappeared? What do you mean?"

Richard sagged in his seat.

I frowned. "She was staying with George and Bella, wasn't she?" I fumbled in his silence. "She's at his London residence, the Herber."

"When I went there yesterday to visit her, George refused to let me see her. This morning I returned with some men-at-arms, determined. We searched the house, but could find her nowhere."

I stared. No. It could not be—

For the first time in many moons, my spine prickled with unease. Nanette was co-heiress with Bella of Warwick's vast estates. Was George preventing Richard from marrying Nanette so he could receive the revenue exclusively for his own use?

Richard lifted his eyes to mine. "Exactly so, Mother. Nanette could not have disappeared of her own accord. George must have hidden her somewhere."

"What do you want me to do?"

"I would like you to talk to George, and Edward if necessary."

"Will the king agree to your marriage?"

"When we won at Tewkesbury, Edward said I could have anything I wanted. I told him I wanted Nanette."

"And?"

Richard met my eyes and smiled in a way that made his face glow. "He roared with laughter and slapped me on the back."

"Where is she?"

George remained silent, his hand clenched around a cup of wine. As usual, he looked magnificent in a ruby-colored tunic, his long sleeves brushing the floor, cut to show off the white velvet undershirt he wore beneath. But he was already on his third cup of wine and it was only mid-morning. At twenty-two, my son was still handsome, but his reddening nose and slackening paunch told of a life that lacked purpose. Edward had pardoned his brother for plotting to take the throne of England. But he kept him on a tight leash and gave him little to do.

I sighed. "My son, this is serious. If anything happened to Nanette, you would be in grave trouble. Edward is testing you."

"Nothing will happen to her!" George interrupted, flushing.

"How do you know that? Do you know where she is?"

I was interrupted by the sound of hooves, of metal clanking, and of male voices shouting. There was a jingle of spurs as someone ran up the stairs.

It was Richard.

I'd never seen him look so angry. He looked exactly as his father had the day he discovered my affair with Blaybourne.

"I cannot believe it!" he shouted. "You took her to a common cook shop where I find her working in the kitchens!"

Flushing crimson, George rose from his seat and fumbled for his dagger.

"*George!*" I said.

It made him stop in his tracks. George had hidden Nanette in a *cook shop*? She had been forced to work in the *kitchens*? George's sense of humor seemed to have become oddly twisted.

"George," I said, "Is this true?"

George flicked his eyes away and pursed his lips.

As he did so, I thanked God silently that I had chosen to live out my declining years as abbess of a Benedictine Order, rather than with George and his family. For something had gone horribly wrong. George was charming, he was intelligent, he was well educated. As a boy, he'd always been my stalwart, defending the family during his father's absence like a bulldog.

What had happened? I'd never known him to behave like this. Had the death of his first child warped him somehow?

"It is true, Mother, I tell you," said Richard. "I went there myself. I saw Nanette with my own eyes. She was disheveled, dirty, and very, very scared. She had given up hope of anyone finding her."

He turned back to George. "What were you trying to do?" he roared. "Murder her? You know Nanette is not strong. Yet she was doing back-breaking work in a fiery kitchen by day and sleeping in a freezing attic by night!"

"George," I said. "How long did you plan to keep her like this?"

"Until Richard left her alone," replied George. He strutted over to his brother, jutting his chin out. "Where is she?"

"I have her in safe keeping."

"I demand that you return her to my house," said George, putting his hands behind his back, which made him look even more like a strutting cock.

Richard clenched his jaw, and his lips thinned.

I hurried over to stand between my sons, putting my hand on Richard's sleeve. "Where is she, my son? Is she safe?"

Richard stopped glaring at his brother. "Have no fear, Mother," he said, patting my arm. "She is safe in Saint Martin-le-Grand in Newgate Street. I have put her into the care of her uncle the Archbishop of York."

Archbishop George Neville was a nephew of mine, the younger brother of Warwick. I had known him all his life. Indeed, he had been one of the children I had been minding in the garden at Bisham when I met my lord Richard as an adult.

"You have done well, my son. How long do you plan to keep her there?"

"Until our marriage takes place," replied Richard.

"No!" roared George.

"You cannot prevent my marriage to Nanette. She is not your ward. Nor can you take her away from our kinsman the archbishop."

"Edward will agree with me," said George, turning to go.

"He'll agree with me," responded Richard, more quietly, following his brother.

❦

Edward, at length, was able to persuade Richard and George to bury their differences. George agreed to the carving-up of Warwick's estates after receiving the greater share of them and was created Earl of Warwick and Salisbury in right of his wife.

On his marriage to Nanette, Richard received Warwick's estates in Yorkshire, Northumberland, and Cumberland, which included Sheriff Hutton and Middleham. Richard and Nanette married in the spring of 1472. They had but one child, a son whom they named Edward after the king.

Chapter 22
1473 to 1478

During this time, my prayers were answered, and George and Bella had more children. Their second child, named Margaret after my daughter, the Duchess of Burgundy, was born August 14, 1473. Their third child, named Edward after the king, was born February 25, 1475.

However, tensions rumbled on between my sons. George and Edward barely tolerated each other, and even Richard grew more critical of the king. In 1475, Richard had gone over to France with the army, ready to give the French another Agincourt. But Edward allowed himself to be bought off by the King of France like a wealthy merchant who will prostitute his services to the highest bidder.

"This is insupportable," Richard told me later. "Edward does not behave as a prince of blood. He cheats us of an honorable peace at Picquigny."

I could only sigh. Every year, Edward did something that seemed to demonstrate his low origins.

In the summer of 1476, Richard finally prevailed upon Edward to re-inter my lord of York in a proper resting place at Fotheringhay. Richard acted as chief mourner and led the seven-day procession from Pontefract – where my lord had been hastily interred after his foul murder – to Fotheringhay.

I wished to be present, of course. But in the end, I begged off, saying it was too painful. The reason was that the Serpent insisted on being there, and Edward was unable or unwilling to say no to her. Richard blamed the delay of the re-internment on Edward's irresponsibility.

I had other things to think of. One day earlier in that year of 1476, I was at my prayers when the steward announced the Duchess of Suffolk. I was surprised; January was a bad time for traveling. I rose at once.

"Mother, dearest!" Beth kissed my cheek as she entered my bedchamber. Her black woolen cloak was covered in snow from the storm outside.

"My dearest child, what has happened?"

"My lord John and our children send you their affectionate greetings. They are well."

"But?"

Beth drew up a chair, and bade me sit.

"Margaret?" I whispered.

"Nan." She sat down beside me, and took my hands. "Nan is dead."

"No."

"Yes, Mother."

Rising swiftly, I nearly knocked over my chair. "No. It can't be true." I folded my arms over my chest and gazed at the white flakes tumbling down outside. "All these years, I've been trying to reach her."

Beth was silent.

"How did she die?"

"In childbirth, Mother."

"Childbirth? I didn't know she was expecting."

"Her daughter Anne died last year, at the age of twenty."

I sank into a chair, my arms wrapped around me, and rocked to and fro. Nan's daughter, Anne Holland, had been married to the Serpent's son Thomas Grey. He'd made her die in childbirth.

"Nan decided to have another child. The child lives and is called Anne St. Leger."

"I didn't know," I whispered. "Was she happy, with her —her lover?"

"They were married, Mother dear," said Beth, chafing my cold hands. "Anne got her divorce three years ago and has been married for two years."

"It's all my fault," I burst out, rising. "I should never have let her go. I'll never forget the day she was torn away from me. If only—"

The rest of the sentence disappeared as I flung myself onto my bed. "If only I'd never met Blaybourne," I sobbed into a pillow, "then Richard would not have punished me with Nan's marriage."

Beth sat by me and held my hand.

"We can't have run out of time." I wept. "I had plans to see her again."

Beth summoned Jenet, who mixed up a potion to help me sleep.

I slept that day. But it was many moons before I slept well again. The sands of time had run through my fingers, and Nan was gone, dead at the age of thirty-six. I paced around my chamber during the dead of night. Why hadn't I done more to reach her? Dark waves of guilt washed over me as I gazed at the stars.

❦

In October 1476, Bella presented George with their fourth child, a son they named Richard. But she never recovered. By mid November, she was so ill, she was taken home to Warwick Castle to die. She passed on just before Christmas 1476, at the age of twenty-five. Their child died ten days later.

George was heartbroken, and I was consumed with worry. Naturally, George wished to marry again, for he had two children under the age of five. His first choice was Mary of Burgundy, now nearly twenty years old. On her father's death in January 1477, she had become the heiress to his vast duchy. But Edward thwarted George at every turn, and the Serpent added fuel to the fire by proposing her own brother Anthony Woodville, Earl Rivers, as bridegroom. In the end, Mary married Maximilian of Austria with Edward's blessing.

George's second choice of bride was Princess Margaret of Scotland. But Edward again forbade the match. Surmising that the Serpent was responsible for these decisions, George decided to strike at her through one of her women, Ankarette Twynho, who'd served Bella before her death. Taking the king's justice into his own hands, George arrested, tried, and executed Dame Twynho on the grounds that she had poisoned Bella, being the means by which the Serpent had put a curse on Bella to make her die.

Edward was furious, but did nothing.

"The king is showing a great deal of forbearance," I remarked, listening to Robert Stillington, the Bishop of Bath and Wells, explain the situation. "You have seen George much of late. How is he?"

Bishop Stillington cleared his throat. "I have some news that I fear will greatly distress you, and that is the reason for my visit."

I gripped the chair handles.

"The Duke of Clarence is publicly declaring the king to be a bastard."

"Not that," I murmured. But of course he would say such a thing. I had taught him to say it, and it was becoming clear that in the wake of Bella's death, George was becoming unhinged.

The bishop signaled to my women. "I fear I have greatly distressed you."

I waved them away and sipped my wine. I must do penance for my sins, and one way I could do that was to hear the worst.

"What else does George say?"

The bishop sighed and lowered his voice: "He declares the king to be a necromancer and says that his marriage to the queen is null and void because tradition forbids the King of England to marry widows."

I shook my head. "George is not well. The death of his wife has been a great shock."

"You might be right, my lady. His actions seemed designed to cause the most offense. Why, yesterday he publicly accused the queen of murdering his duchess by poison and sorcery. And he refuses to eat or drink anything at court."

My hands trembled as I put my wine-cup down. "What of the king?" I whispered.

"He is very patient with his brother."

❦

But that could not last much longer. As I paced my chamber that night, gazing at the moon, I could imagine the Serpent's reaction:

"I tell you, he's gone quite mad," she would say. "He thinks he can do anything he likes, such as storming into your council chamber and demanding that the king's justice be overturned."

Edward would sigh. It was true that George was becoming a problem, but he was loath to act. His brother was amusing. And they were both so alike, much more so than their youngest brother Richard. "George has no real power. He is greatly upset by his wife's death."

"Edward! He's dangerous. Don't you remember how he plotted against you with Warwick? But worst of all is what he's said against me. He says I'm not your legitimate wife!"

"No one takes him seriously."

"Sweeting, think about this. If Clarence believes I'm not your legitimate wife, then what is he going to think about our children? He's going to say they are bastards. And so he'll not allow our Edward to inherit the throne. What say you to that?"

"You have a point there."

"And so you will see to it that Clarence is removed, won't you, my sweeting?"

❦

And so it came to pass that George was incarcerated in the Tower of London. Months passed and Edward did nothing. Then, he summoned Parliament to meet in January 1478 to try George publicly for his offenses.

"I have a copy of the attainder with me."

The Archbishop of Canterbury, Thomas Bourchier, handed me his scroll and bowed. Thomas Bourchier, a kinsman-by-marriage of my lord husband Richard, had been chosen by Richard to be Archbishop of Canterbury when he was regent of England. Over the years, we had developed a close friendship.

"Pray be seated," I said, "and read it to me. My eyes are tired today." I sat opposite him in front of the fireplace, my face concealed by shadows.

The Archbishop cleared his throat. "The king read the indictment himself. He accused his brother, George,

Duke of Clarence, of new treasons to exalt himself and his heir to the regality of the crown of England. He said that he had ever loved and cherished his brother, giving him so large a portion of possessions that seldom had been seen. The duke's love, for all this, did not increase but grew daily more and more in malice. He falsely and traitorously intended the destruction and disinheriting of the king and his issue."

I put my hand in front of my face as the Archbishop stopped. I could not deny the charges. And, yet, Edward had never handled George well. What would have happened if George had been allowed to have a position in Edward's cabinet? Would he have used it to try and take the throne that way?

"What will happen now?"

"The Lords and the Commons demand that the sentence be carried out."

I gripped the chair so hard, my knuckles went white. If that were true, George would suffer the full horrors of a traitor's death, the hanging, the drawing, and the quartering. Couldn't Edward lock him up for the duration of his lifetime? But Edward had done that for Henry of Lancaster, only to find he became the focus of opposition. Henry of Lancaster had been removed, a threat to Edward's throne.

I pinched my lips together and rose, then wobbled. The Archbishop rushed to put a hand under my elbow. I sank into my seat.

"I must write to the king."

Dear Edward, I wrote, *Archbishop Bourchier has told me that George has been indicted on charges of treason. I beg you not to let him die a traitor's death. I humbly request that you commute the sentence to a beheading, or some other way preferred by George, and that you allow it to be done privately to spare our family further scandal.*

In sorrow, Cecylee, Duchess of York.

I gazed out of the window. It was bitter cold, and I struggled to keep my heavy fur wrap around me as I stood there, sleepless. Dawn came, black changing to grey and white. It was February 19, 1478, a cold day under the clouds, snow falling. Wisps of chill damp infected my bones as I knelt to pray for the soul of my son George.

Had he been executed the night before?

What had become of him?

I was near unto sixty-three years, yet hours went by as I continued to fast and pray, moving my lips over the prayers composed by Saint Bridget of Sweden:

> *O Jesu, endless sweetness of all that love thee, a joy passing and exceeding all gladness and desire, the savior and lover of all repentant sinners ...*

A voice softly said, "Mother?"

Slowly, I opened my eyes and through my cloudy vision a face gradually came into focus. The face seemed to be George's. But it dissolved and became Richard's. I'd never noticed Richard to be like George before.

I tried to move, but could not.

Someone lifted me up and gently set me into my favorite chair. The room came to life as folk stoked up the fire and bustled around with cups of mulled wine and refreshments.

"I cannot eat," I murmured.

Richard sat down beside me. "I'll not have you go as well."

An image of George the day I'd faced down the Lancastrian army at Ludlow filled my head. How bright and handsome he'd looked in his suit of green and gold, chosen especially to match my outfit. He showed little fear, even when the army burst into town, staring at everything with his unusual blue-green eyes. And now I would never see him again.

"Mother," came a voice. "Mother, where are you?"

"George?" I murmured. Someone's warm hands picked mine up, and Richard's face wavered into view. "You must eat, Mother. You'll make yourself ill if you do not."

I took my handkerchief out of my sleeve and dabbed my eyes. A procession of people filled my mind's eye: my beloved Joan, my lost daughter Nan, my murdered child Edmund, my lord husband Richard, and my dearest friend and confidante, Mama. I sagged in my seat, bone weary. Truly, I was living a long and unhappy life. Lisette's curse had come true. Maybe if I continued to fast, I could see Mama again.

But Richard was by my side once more. He cut a small morsel of my favorite honey wafer, put it on a plate. Then he stared me down until I took a nibble. He handed me my wine cup and used the power of his blue-grey eyes to encourage me to take a sip.

"You're so quiet, Mother."

I lifted my eyes. "George?"

Richard slumped in his seat and took my hands. "He's gone."

"How?"

"I'm not going to tell you."

I stared at my hands as tears slipped past my lids and down my cheeks. I was responsible for George's death. By announcing the king's illegitimacy in front of everyone, I provided the motive to turn against his brother. George had always been intensely jealous of Edward, but I refused to see that. I believed I could manage George, but he was unstable and easily led.

What a sin I had committed by being unfaithful to my lord. Edward was not legitimate, but he'd executed the legitimate heir. What had I done? What monster had I brought into our family?

I stared into Richard's blue-grey eyes. Was I with my lord? No. Richard was the only son left to me, and I must protect him. I sat up in my chair.

"What will you do?"

"I've been loyal to Edward," replied Richard. "And will continue so while he lives. But I owe no loyalty to his wife, nor to her numerous relations."

"The queen is dangerous," I remarked, rising. "Remember what happened when she stole the king's signet ring and had the Earl of Desmond and his two young children executed? And all because he made some unfortunate—and very true—remarks about the king's choice of a wife."

Richard glanced at me. "I'd forgotten that."

"You are next," I said, going to him. "Mark my words, if she has any excuse to rid herself of you, she will."

"I'm determined to fight for what is rightfully ours," he said. "And you must be determined, Mother, not to let George's ... death get you down."

"You've given me hope," I replied, as I blessed him.

❦

I do not know what happened to darling George. He died in mysterious circumstances in the Tower on the night of February 18, 1478. Some say he drowned in a barrel of Malmsey wine. But I preferred to think that he died the more dignified death of beheading by an expert swordsman.

Poor George was buried in Tewkesbury Abbey, next to his wife Bella.

Five years passed. The country seemed to be at peace.

Until one day, in early April 1483.

Chapter 23
March to April 1483

I knew nothing of these events until much later, for the Serpent neglected to tell me.

Edward loved fishing and had insisted on going out on a boat in the cold, blustery, wet weather of March 1483. It was not surprising that he caught a chill and had to take to his bed. But everyone expected him to recover, for he was only forty years old.

However, Edward was as intemperate in his eating habits as he was with his mistresses. Gone was the lean, muscular, and handsome youth crowned king at the age of eighteen. In his place was a man with an enormous stomach, who frequently purged himself for the pleasure of gorging on food and drink.

The Serpent summoned a horde of doctors, to no avail. Edward died on the ninth day of April.

❦

If she did not act quickly, the Serpent's hold on power would disappear. Her first aim was to get her eldest son, twelve-year-old Edward, Prince of Wales, to London, where he would be under her care. For when his father died, the prince was some two hundred miles away at Ludlow. Fortunately, she'd used her charms to convince Edward to give the guardianship of his heir to her brother, Anthony Woodville, Earl Rivers, whose loyalty to her was unquestioned.

Her second aim was to deal with the king's younger brother, Richard of Gloucester, immensely powerful in the north of England partly because he owned an enormous amount of land and partly because he had the power to dispense the king's justice. It was imperative to keep the king's condition secret from Gloucester, because Edward had named him Protector of the Realm until Prince Edward reached his majority.

But if Prince Edward were brought to his mother in London, he could be crowned immediately, and there would be no need for Gloucester to act as Protector.

The Serpent loathed and feared Gloucester, for he was close to me and, like me, had disapproved of Edward's marriage. Unlike George, Richard was crafty enough to keep his feelings to himself. But he'd made his displeasure with the Woodvilles plain by rarely coming to court.

The Serpent lost no time, apprising Rivers of Edward's death and urging him to bring the young prince to London.

To the late king's mother and younger brother, she wrote not a word, hoping we would not learn of Edward's death until it was too late.

Chapter 24
April 11 to 17, 1483

To Cecylee, Duchess of York, Greetings.
Madam,

It has come to my attention that you may not have been apprised of the sad news of the late king's passing, here in London, on the ninth day of April. You should also know it was the late king's wish that his brother, Richard, Duke of Gloucester, be Protector of the Realm until such time as Prince Edward reaches his majority.

Written this eleventh day of April, in the year 1483,
Thomas Bourchier, Archbishop of Canterbury.

I sagged and dropped the letter. Edward dead? How could that be? He was only forty years old, and he was a vital, larger-than-life person whose ringing laugh made even the sourest person merry. Whatever had happened?

I sat in my chair for many moments, hearing the vast silence of his absence. I no longer went to court and had not seen him in years. My sons and daughters communicated with letters and visits. All except Edward, who never visited, and rarely wrote. Over the years, I'd only been able to glean news of him from others.

But he was my son, and had been a daily presence in my thoughts for the past forty years. Despite his irresponsibility and lack of taste, he'd been a strong king. He held everything together, keeping the factions of his government at bay by giving Richard power in the north while the Serpent's family had their power base in the south.

Now what would happen?

The Serpent was well placed to seize power, for she was in London, and her relatives had been rewarded with positions in Edward's government. I gripped the arms of my chair.

What was going to become of Richard?

If the Serpent prevailed, she would strip him of his offices. She would take away his land and his home. She would leave him with nothing.

But she would not end there. No. She would find some way to incarcerate him in the Tower.

I picked up the Archbishop's letter. It was written two days after Edward's death. Had anyone told my remaining son? It reminded me of the time when Henry of Lancaster had gone mad, and the Bitch of Anjou had kept the news from Richard of York.

I sat up suddenly, berating myself for the sluggishness of my mind. Of course the Serpent would not want Richard of Gloucester to know about his brother's death! I must write to him at once!

To Richard, Duke of Gloucester, Greetings.

Dearest Richard,

I write in haste to tell you that Edward the King passed away suddenly this ninth day of April. I have a subtle suspicion that the Serpent may not have apprised you of this news, and so I urge you to move swiftly to protect your interests. Perhaps you should have Prince Edward transferred to your care.

Written this thirteenth day of April 1483,

Your loving mother, Cecylee, Duchess of York.

While I anxiously waited for a reply from Richard, the Serpent held her first council meeting. First, she asked for a new bidding prayer to be said in the churches. This was customary on the death of a sovereign, but the Serpent had purposely worded it so that the name of Richard of Gloucester was left out.

The king's council should have voted this down, but it was packed with her friends and relations. There was the Archbishop of York and the Bishop of Ely, who had been friends of the king and queen. There was her eldest son, Thomas Grey, first Marquess of Dorset, who had control of the king's treasure and the royal ordinance. And then there were the aristocrats her sisters had married.

They agreed with the Serpent.

They agreed too when the Serpent requested they proclaim Edward Prince of Wales, King of England.

But when the Serpent requested that the coronation take place as soon as possible, William Hastings, the Lord Chamberlain and Edward's closest friend, objected.

"Why so hasty?" he demanded. "King Edward has a protector-designate."

It turned out that Edward had altered his will at the last minute to say that his brother of Gloucester should be protector-designate until Prince Edward reached his majority. The Serpent was not happy.

She turned to the Archbishop of Canterbury, because he would officiate at the coronation. "What say you, my lord?"

Thomas Bourchier smiled slightly. "Perhaps it would be more prudent to wait."

"We've just declared war on France," remarked Dorset. "I think it would be wise to have a smooth transition. Crowning Prince Edward now would show the French that matters have not changed."

Smiling, the Serpent consulted her scroll. "What say you, my lords, to Sunday, the fourth day of May?"

They agreed.

The Serpent then requested that twelve-year-old Edward be escorted the hundred miles from Ludlow to London by an army of soldiers.

"An army!" exclaimed Hastings. "Whom in this realm do you fear so much?"

"The king should have a suitable escort," remarked Dorset, allowing the Serpent to evade the question.

"But not an army!" shouted Hastings. "It will only sow trouble and bloodshed."

"I want no harm to befall my son," replied the Serpent.

"If you insist on this foolhardy whim, madam," replied Hastings, "then I'll retire to Calais."

This was no empty threat, for Hastings was the Governor of Calais, and it was from Calais that Warwick had plotted his coup against Edward.

"I suggest, madam," continued Hastings, "that you limit the prince's escort to two thousand men."

The Serpent looked around the table, but the king's councilors would not meet her gaze. She was forced to abandon her plan.

She summoned her scribe and wrote to her brother Rivers for a second time, urging him to bring the prince quickly to London.

❦

A few days passed, then I received Richard's reply:

Dearest Mother,

I thank you most heartily for your message. Indeed, no one had thought to apprise me of this situation, saving yourself and Hastings. I agree with your suggestion concerning Prince Edward's person. If we do not win, we will be in grave jeopardy for the reasons that you well know.

Written this seventeenth day of April 1483

Your loving son,

R. Gloucester

I smiled; Richard's plans were already well in hand. I fingered my rosary beads. The next few days would determine who would win, and it would be hard to wait. I rang my bell. I would summon my women and design a new altar cloth, which we would sew. And I would ask Master Gerard to ensure that we had a goodly supply of wine, for I found it most comforting in the evenings when the shadows drew in.

I was going to need all the comfort I could find.

Chapter 25
April 20th to May 7th 1483

By the greatest good fortune, the Serpent's brother Rivers planned to celebrate Saint George's Day in Ludlow and saw no reason to alter his plans. He ignored his sister's urgent pleas and did not leave Ludlow until the morning of April 24. This gave Richard a week to muster his forces before marching south.

Richard arrived in York on April 20 and sent out messengers to ascertain where the young king was. His plan was to intercept Rivers before he arrived in London. Fortunately, Rivers took his time. He did not arrive in Northampton with his charge until April 29.

> *I had a prior undertaking to meet with Rivers in Northampton,* wrote Richard to me, *but he tried to slip through my fingers. Instead of staying there, he rode on another fourteen miles to Stony Stratford and found lodgings for the prince there. He then rode back to meet Buckingham and myself.*

I put the letter down and frowned. Henry Stafford, second Duke of Buckingham? What was Richard doing with him?

Buckingham was my great-nephew but had not been popular at Edward's court, being jealous, proud, and ruthlessly ambitious. He'd never bothered to conceal his hatred of the queen, who had forced him to marry one of her sisters. He harbored a grudge against the King because of a dispute over some estates. He was, I realized with dismay, not unlike George. If Buckingham had now switched his allegiance to Richard's cause, it could only be because he hoped that Richard would reward him for his loyalty by returning the disputed Bohun estates. Did Richard know this?

I picked up Richard's letter:

> *When Rivers arrived in Northampton with the queen dowager's second son, Sir Richard Grey, I received them graciously, and asked them to sup with me. I considered it wise*

not to betray my anger at River's gross presumption at lodging the king so far away without consulting me first. Over dinner, I gently pumped Rivers for information, and he acquainted me with the dealings of the council in London. Suffice it to say, there appeared to be no place for me in the new king's government.

You may realize, dear Mother, how alarmed I was. But I concealed my feelings behind smiles and gestures of goodwill. That night, Rivers and Grey slept in the accommodation I had arranged for them in Northampton, while Buckingham and I posted guards around that inn and along the road leading to Stony Stratford.

The next day, at dawn, Buckingham and I rode to Stony Stratford at full speed with Sir Richard Grey. The king was full pleased to see us, so we dismissed his escort and his attendants and set off for Northampton.

"Madam."

I looked up as my steward bowed.

"A messenger has arrived from London."

I put Richard's letter down. "What is the news?"

"The queen dowager has taken sanctuary in Westminster Abbey
with her five daughters, two of her four sons, and her brother, the Bishop of Salisbury," replied the messenger, kneeling before me.

Had Richard already succeeded in crushing the Woodvilles? But he was not yet in London. Or was this a clever ruse by the Serpent to make her look powerless and thus to gain sympathy? For she was not powerless at all. She was like a spider spinning a web.

I motioned for the messenger to continue.

"Your son, Richard, Duke of Gloucester, has imprisoned Rivers in Sheriff Hutton, Sir Richard Grey in Middleham, and others of their affinity in Pontefract."

By Our Lady, Richard had moved with lightning speed.

"When my lord duke was informed that the Archbishop of York had given the Great Seal of England to the queen, he removed him from office."

I smiled grimly and let out a breath. Archbishop Thomas Rotherham was known to be a staunch friend of the queen. Richard had performed magnificently. I picked up his letter again.

"What do the people say?"

The messenger coughed and looked at the ground. "Unfortunately, madam, they murmur that these actions are those of a tyrant."

I stared at him. Motioning for the messenger to leave, I ignored the prickle of unease that crept up my spine and the painful memories of my lord Richard's bid for power.

> *I am proceeding onto London with my nephew. And, madam, I beseech you to throw off your present cares and go to Baynard's Castle, your residence in London, so that I may take counsel with you to my comfort.*
>
> *Written at Northampton, the second day of May, with the hand of your most humble son,*
>
> *R. Gloucester*

❦

On the third of May, Richard of Gloucester set off for London in the company of his cousin Henry of Buckingham and the young King Edward V.

On the fourth of May, they entered London, and Gloucester lodged the prince in the palace of the bishops of London.

On the seventh of May, the Archbishop of Canterbury, on Gloucester's orders, recovered the Great Seal of England from the queen dowager.

Chapter 26
Baynard's Castle, London
May 7, 1483

What would happen to Richard when King Edward V gained his majority? My grandson already had twelve years. We didn't have long to act, for a precedent had been set by Henry of Lancaster, who'd declared his majority at sixteen.

If we did nothing, Edward would reward his numerous Woodville relatives once he came of age.

Thus, it was imperative we invalidated the will of the late king immediately. And so I summoned my dear friend Thomas Bourchier, Archbishop of Canterbury, to a private meeting at Baynard's Castle.

"My lord," he said when Richard explained what we intended to do, "everything is in order. The late king's will has been properly signed and sealed. What objections do you have?"

I took a deep breath. "There are things you know not, my lord Archbishop. Things that cause me great sorrow."

Richard signaled and a servant brought me wine.

I sipped it slowly before continuing. "Long ago, when I was young, I sinned grievously against my lord husband. I bore a child that was not his."

There was a long silence as I thought of all that had gone wrong.

The archbishop leaned forward. "Are you speaking, my lady, of the late king?"

I nodded.

"You are quite certain, Lady Cecylee, that this is so?"

"I am willing to swear on holy relics," I replied.

The archbishop put his hands inside his long, wide sleeves, and considered.

"If it be true that Lord Edward was indeed illegitimate, then he should have been debarred from ascending the throne of England. Thus we have grounds for declaring his will to be illegal."

He turned to me. "Because you alone, Lady Cecylee, can answer that question, I believe it more politic if you would sign the statement declaring Lord Edward's will to be invalid."

Richard summoned a scribe, who drew up the document.

"What do you intend to do about Lord Edward's sons?" asked the archbishop in a low tone.

"I have not made a decision as yet," replied Richard. "Their mother is a dangerous schemer. I intend to deal with her, and with them, at a time and place of my own choosing."

On the tenth of May, Richard was made Lord Protector of England.

Chapter 27
Baynard's Castle, London
May 26, 1483

Richard sat tense in my big throne-like chair, taut as a harp string, turning his signet ring round and around. Any more of this and he would snap.

"My conscience has tormented me for years," said our guest, Robert Stillington, Bishop of Bath and Wells. "But I made a promise to my king and liege lord, to your son, madam, that I would breathe no word of this to any living person."

I pressed a cup of mulled wine into Richard's hand and indicated a seat for the good bishop. The man was haggard with exhaustion, having traveled all the way from his seat at Wells, a distance of some one hundred miles.

"What has tormented you?" I asked, signaling to the servants to bring more wine.

"Madam. I ought to warn you. What I am about to say may horrify you and your son." He bowed to Richard.

I sat wearily in my chair, indicating to the servants to leave the flagon of wine and close the door.

"I know the late king's marriage to Dame Élisabeth Grey caused your family great pain," continued Bishop Stillington as soon as the door shut. "Perhaps it might have caused even greater pain had you known he was already married."

Richard recoiled in his chair. My hands shook so, I spilled some drops of wine.

I busied myself with my handkerchief, cleaning the spill away. Finally, I said, "Edward committed bigamy?"

"Yes, madam."

"Who was the lady?" asked Richard.

"Lady Eleanor Butler."

I put my wine-cup down. "Not Lady Eleanor Talbot, the Earl of Shrewsbury's daughter?"

"Yes, madam. She was married to Sir Thomas Butler, Lord Sudeley's heir, some thirty years ago. I do not know exactly when her husband died, save that he'd passed on by March 1461, when first I met the lady."

I sat back in my seat, turning the cup in my hands. My head filled with an image of Eleanor, a child of such striking beauty back in Rouen. The youngest daughter of my dearest friend Margaret, she had hair the color of silver and deep violet eyes. She had been a quiet child with surprising flashes of naughtiness. Most of all, she'd been the playmate of my beloved Joan.

I blinked away tears as the image changed and six-year-old Eleanor ran through the gardens of Rouen Castle hand in hand with three-year-old Joan.

Someone bent over me. It was Richard.

He chafed my hands. "You look pale, Mother," he murmured. He turned to the bishop. "My lady mother is distressed. Perhaps you should return."

At once, Bishop Stillington was on his feet, his face creased with concern. "Madam, I am more sorry that I can say to bring you such news."

I waved him back to his seat. "What you have told me is very shocking. Edward told me nothing of this—"

I broke off as I remembered something Edward had said. What was it? I grasped at a thread of memory. It had been around the time Warwick and I had been negotiating his marriage with Bona of Savoy. Yes, he'd asked if his bride-to-be had silver hair and violet eyes.

Richard returned to his seat. "Tell us how this happened, when it took place and how you know about it."

"After the death of her husband, Lady Eleanor went to the King to ask him to return her manors. Her father-in-law, Lord Sudeley, had settled two manors on her at the time of her marriage, but after his son's death he wanted one of them back. However, his lordship did not complete the required documents to transfer the title. At that point, King Edward seized her lands, because the Butlers were

Lancastrians who had fought against him. Lady Eleanor was forced to move in with her father-in-law.

"Shortly afterwards, she made her way to the Palace of Windsor to plead her case before the king. He was enchanted by her beauty. Lady Eleanor, however, rebuffed his advances, saying that she would not lie with him unless he married her."

"When did the marriage take place?" asked Richard.

"April of 1462."

I looked at the bishop. When did Easter Sunday fall that year? For it was customary for the Church to ban marriages during the Lenten season.

"How do you know this?" asked Richard.

"I was the officiating priest."

I grasped the handles of my chair and rose. "How could this have happened without my knowledge?"

The bishop went off into a coughing fit.

Richard filled his wine cup and motioned for him to continue.

"I married them in a private ceremony at a Carmelite house in Oxford. There were no witnesses."

I sank into my sear. "Are you saying that her lady mother did not know of this?"

The bishop nodded.

Richard leaned forward in his chair. "Why was the marriage kept so secret?"

The bishop bowed his head. "Lady Eleanor was deeply spiritual. She was beautiful both inside and out. She felt she'd sinned by agreeing to a clandestine marriage with Lord Edward. She was greatly distressed to find herself expecting a child shortly after the marriage took place. She went into seclusion at the Augustinian priory of Wigmore, where she gave birth to a son."

"A son!" exclaimed Richard.

"Yes, my lord. A son named Edward after his father. The child was known as Edward of Wigmore."

"Why did no one say anything?" demanded Richard.

"Lady Eleanor made Lord Edward take a vow of silence. She felt she had wronged her family, wronged her mother, wronged you, my lady," he turned towards me. "She had great respect and love for both her mother and you," he bowed to me. "She did not want power for herself, and she disliked court life. She doubted her ability to be Lord Edward's queen. She wanted only safety and security for herself and her son."

"But if she had come to court as Edward's acknowledged lady and queen, the whole tone of the court would have been different," I said. What would have happened? Would Edward have been as greedy and debauched, lazy, and irresponsible? Maybe not. For I always thought that the Serpent's greed and selfishness brought out the worst in him.

Richard glanced at me, motioning for the bishop to continue.

"Lord Edward tried to change Lady Eleanor's mind, but he could not wait forever."

"And then another Lancastrian widow came along," I put in.

"Indeed," said the bishop. "When Lady Eleanor heard of Lord Edward's marriage to Dame Grey, she was heart-sick. But after her hesitations, she did not feel it right to put forward her own claim. She entered the Carmelite priory at Ludlow."

"Is she alive?" I asked.

"No. She was buried on the thirtieth of June 1468. Truly, I believe, she died of a broken heart."

"What of her son?" asked Richard.

"The child did not survive her."

I rose and walked to the window to hide tears. How different everything could have been.

The bishop coughed. "Of course," he added, "this does have implications."

I turned.

"Since Lord Edward was previously married, his marriage to Dame Grey was unlawful," said Bishop

Stillington. "And so the children of that union are not legitimate, thus have no claim to the throne of England."

I glared. Had Edward let me ruin my reputation rather than admit he was a bigamist? Had he been laughing behind his hand while I struggled with the Serpent? What about all those freezing winters spent in a residence that did not have glazed windows? Or my years of remorse following my outburst?

I had gone through all that humiliation so that Edward could keep his secret. He must have kept it well, for the Serpent could not have known.

The bishop rose and made a deep bow to Richard. "You, my lord," he said, "are the rightful King of England."

Richard's face went quiet.

I looked up. Richard was the most sensitive of my children, the one with the finest mind. He could read Latin fluently and was exceedingly familiar with the laws of the land, having acted as Edward's Justiciar for the past twelve years. He would be a superb king, for he was just and would use his knowledge of the law to protect his people. But he was so modest, so unlike Edward and George.

"I did not look for this," said Richard eventually.

"No you did not," I replied. "But it is yours by right. You know you can do it, for what is kingship if not administering justice to all people?"

Chapter 28
Early June 1483

Richard immediately went about securing his claim to the throne. He didn't have much time, for the coronation of Edward's bastard son had been set for Saint John's Day, less than one month away.

On the fifth day of June, my son moved from Baynard's Castle to his own town house at Crosby Place in Bishopsgate, allowing him secret meetings with those of the king's council who supported him, while continuing to hold open meetings either at my residence or at Westminster. During the open meetings, my son took control of daily matters of the government, permitting my grandson's coronation to go ahead.

But things did not proceed smoothly. For some unaccountable reason, Hastings saw fit to go over to the Woodvilles. I suppose I shouldn't have been surprised, for Hastings was an unsavory character who'd led Edward into the depths of debauchery. Naturally, it was Hastings who'd suggested the boating outing that resulted in Edward's death. Folk said that they even shared mistresses.

On the ninth of June, Richard discovered Hastings plotting with the Serpent to remove him as Lord Protector. Up until that point, Richard hadn't disturbed the Serpent's sanctuary. But it was now imperative that Richard gain custody of Prince Edward's younger brother, the Duke of York, before the Serpent could do further damage. To do this, Richard hit upon the clever idea of bringing forward the date of the coronation by two days to June 22, giving reason to place the young Duke of York in the Tower with his brother, the new king. If the king's brother were not allowed to appear at his coronation, even the Serpent would be embarrassed.

On the tenth of June, Richard wrote to the great northern magnates and the civic council in York, telling them of the Woodville plots and asking for arms and men.

On the eleventh of June, he ordered the executions of Rivers, Grey, and others of their affinity, ensuring that the Woodvilles did not regain power.

On the thirteenth of June, he divided the council. The open meeting met in Westminster and was ordered to finalize plans for the coronation. Richard's secret meeting took place in the Tower. During that, he publicly accused Hastings of treason and had him executed on the spot, without a trial.

Folk will wonder why he did this. After all, Hastings was a nobleman, and the law said he had to be tried by his peers. But Hastings was a dangerous enemy, the Serpent's henchman, and spy.

On the sixteenth of June, Archbishop Bourchier went with many others to the sanctuary to confront the Serpent. They conveyed my son's request that nine-year-old Richard, Duke of York, be removed to the Tower. The Serpent expressed some reservations about her sons' safety. However, our kinsman Bourchier was able to calm her fears, and she handed over her youngest son.

I breathed a sigh of relief upon hearing the news. The Woodvilles were being stripped of their power, and all seemed much easier than I'd dared hope.

On that day, my son took up residence in the royal lodgings at the Tower. Shortly afterwards, the two boys were moved to the inner apartments. They were never seen again.

Chapter 29
June, 1483

It was now time for Richard to explain things to the good people of London.

"My son," I said, "You must tell them of my sin. How else can you claim the throne? If you don't explain that Edward was illegitimate, they will think you are usurping it."

"But, Mother, it would ruin your reputation, and for a lady of your years—"

"It is imperative that you get the Serpent out of the way," I said, interrupting. "And the only way to do that is to claim the throne of England for yourself. But you must get the backing of the Londoners. You cannot expect them to give you the throne, for they think it belongs to your nephew, whom they call *Edward V*."

There was a long pause. Richard got up and went to the window so that I couldn't see his face. But I could tell he was struggling mightily, for he twisted his ring and fiddled with his dagger.

Finally he turned around. "If you're sure, Mother?"

I glanced down. This was not going to be easy. Women who erred were not treated kindly, and I was not looking forward to the effect these revelations would have. But I had to crush the Serpent. I lifted my chin. "I am sure."

❦

But Richard procrastinated and allowed the coronation arrangements for my grandson to continue. He did not show his hand until Sunday, June 22, the day of the presumed coronation. Naturally, the Londoners were buzzing with anticipation.

Doctor Ralph Shaw of Cambridge University preached a sermon at Saint Paul's Cross in which he told everyone that Edward IV was illegitimate. Naturally, I was not present, and so I had to hear about it from members of my household. I thought that telling the truth about my sins would help my son Richard become king. But my informants told me something surprising. When Doctor Shaw made these allegations, the crowd became silent. When their murmurs eventually started up, it became apparent they didn't believe him.

Now it was my turn to be surprised. Why wouldn't folk believe it, especially as it happened to be true? I was not prepared for this. According to my informants—and I had many—people didn't believe that someone as pious as I could have sinned so greatly.

It was true that I heard Mass several times a day, and that I was a Benedictine abbess. But I never thought of myself as more saintly than others. If only they knew! I was pious *because* I had sinned so greatly.

I was dismayed: Everyone knew the Londoners had to be on your side if you were to govern England effectively. What was going to happen to Richard?

❦

"They didn't believe you." I exclaimed. "Why not?"

Richard sighed. In the pearly light of an early summer evening, he looked grey and drawn. "I don't know," he replied sinking into one of my chairs. "What should I do now?"

I folded my arms. "Edward was always popular with the Londoners. It was the source of his power.

"Where does that put me, Mother?"

"They will know you in good time, my son. Meanwhile, you must develop a new strategy. It seems you are going to have to drop the story of Edward's illegitimacy, it is doing you more harm than good."

"What can I say?"

"Tell them the story of Lady Eleanor," I replied. "If they have difficulty in believing a pious old woman could produce an illegitimate son, they will have a much easier time believing that Edward was a bigamist. After all, they knew what he was like with women."

"That's true." Richard rose stiffly from his chair. "Why did I not think of that before?"

I put my hand on his shoulder, which felt fragile and bony to my touch. "Because you're exhausted," I said. "And you have not been nourishing yourself for these past several weeks."

❦

Richard took my advice, and that very same day sent his cousin Henry Stafford, Duke of Buckingham, to the Guildhall to address the mayor, aldermen and citizens of London.

Buckingham spoke eloquently on my son's behalf, glossing over my foolishness and instead telling the good people about Edward's bigamous marriage with Lady Eleanor. He ended by appealing to them to offer the crown to my son Richard.

Again, they were met by that silence. Apparently, people were not happy about the way Hastings had been executed without trial. They were not happy that Richard had not crowned his nephew as promised. They were very unhappy that he had a large army in the north that he could bring down on them at any moment. For they hadn't forgotten how they'd suffered under the Bitch of Anjou.

I sighed with impatience, but trusted Richard's sterling qualities would sway them.

Buckingham remedied the situation by having his men throw their caps into the air and shout, "King Richard!"

The next day, there was a meeting of the Lords and Commons in Westminster. Again, Buckingham addressed them, dwelling on Edward's bigamy with Lady Eleanor. And so they declared Edward's marriage to the Serpent to be invalid, their children illegitimate.

Richard's reign had begun, and I could finally retire in peace.

For my work was done.

Chapter 30
July 1483

My youngest son, King Richard III, dated his reign from June 26, 1483, the day he was installed on the King's Bench in Westminster Hall. He now had the title Richard, Duke of York, had striven for, the title that had been torn from him by his enemies in 1460. It was my son's task to ensure that he kept that title.

Richard was crowned in Westminster Abbey on July 6, 1483, in the presence of his beloved wife Nanette, who was crowned queen, and their only son and heir, Edward of Middleham. I was not present, not because I disapproved of Richard as certain folk claim, but because I was indisposed, the strain of the previous weeks finally coming home to roost.

However, I rose from my bed to give the new king my solemn blessing before he set out for his coronation.

Richard was anxious that his subjects should know their new king, so only two weeks after his coronation, he set off on a royal progress to travel around the country. He'd been traveling only three days when he decided to pay me a sudden visit early one morning.

"My son," I said, coming forward and searching his face. "What troubles you?"

Richard had acquired a healthy summer tan, but dark circles around his eyes betokened many restless nights.

"Come with me," I added, "and let us pray for guidance."

We went to my private chapel. It was a spare, white-washed room with a portrait of Saint Bridget and a statue of Our Lady carrying the Lord Jesus. The king and I spent the next several minutes in prayer.

Afterwards, I led Richard back to the solar, now warmed by a roaring fire. Richard had been kind enough to restore all of my lands, and so I was able to entertain in rather better style than previously. I signaled to the steward to open my best Bordeaux, which I poured for him myself. Then I settled in a large carved chair with cushions and rug.

Richard put his wine cup down untouched, covering his face with one hand. I signaled for Mother Avisa to get a tonic for headaches.

Then:

"Those accursed Woodvilles," he finally spat. "Am I never to be free of their plotting?"

I frowned at the rawness of his outburst. His life had not been easy of late, and he needed rest. Otherwise he would damage his health.

He looked up. "Two plots have I uncovered: One is to spirit Edward's daughters out of their sanctuary in Westminster Abbey and send them abroad. The other is to rescue Edward's sons from the Tower."

"No." I put my wine cup down.

"Indeed yes, Mother," he replied.

I rose stiffly to my feet and went to put a hand on his shoulder. My son ached for comfort, I could feel it. "We must act decisively to stop this nonsense once and for all," I said. "We cannot lose heart now. You are the legitimate ruler of England. No one can take that away from you."

I sat next to him and chafed his hands. "As for Edward's daughters, all you need do is tighten your cordon around Westminster Abbey. You have enough men for the task. You must insist no one goes in or out of the abbey without your permission."

"What should I do about Edward's sons?"

I paused, for that was a knotty problem.

"We should plan for the future," I replied. "Of all my children, only Edward, Beth, George, and you have male heirs. George's son, Edward, Earl of Warwick, also has a claim to the throne, but he is only eight years old. He is too young and not strong enough in his wits to be a real threat to you as long as you keep him with a trusted member of the family. Perhaps you should have him stay with Nanette, as she is his nearest female relation. The poor child needs some kindness in his life, and your wife will be kind.

Richard's smile wiped away his lines.

"Beth has many sons, all strong and healthy," I continued. "And more to the point, they are loyal to you. If anything happened to your boy, perhaps you should consider making her eldest, John de la Pole, Earl of Lincoln, your heir."

The color drained from Richard's face.

I took his hands. "Richard, I know you find this painful, but we live in dangerous times. Your Edward is only seven years old, and not strong. Beth's eldest son has twenty-one years, old enough to assume the responsibility of being your heir. He can fight for you."

Richard made a face as I pressed a wine glass into his hands. He took a sip and put it down. "What about Edward's sons?"

"Folk do not want to believe they're bastards," I replied. "The Serpent and her horde of Woodville relatives will never stop plotting. Edward's sons are Woodvilles at heart, their mother saw to that. Edward was too weak-willed to stop her. As Woodvilles, they pose a danger to your throne. You've already discovered one plot. There will be others."

Richard nodded, and we gazed at the fire together.

"How I blame myself," I said, "for my own lack of responsibility. If Edward had not been born, none of this would have happened."

"Edward seemed like a hero to me when I was a boy," murmured Richard.

I winced. "The plain truth is that he and I were too much alike. I was irresponsible in the getting of him, and he was irresponsible in his marriages, particularly in bringing that awful Woodville woman into the family. His fault compounded my own. The worm in the apple was his wife, his *second* wife."

Richard was silent.

I leaned forward. "For the good of our family and for the good of England, we must set right these wrongs." I took both his hands in mine and gazed into his eyes. "We must destroy the Woodvilles once and for all."

Richard stared at me. "Do you really believe that?" he whispered. "Rid ourselves of those two boys in the Tower?"

I paused for a long moment. I could hardly believe what I was suggesting, but what could I do? The Serpent was dangerous.

"It grieves me much that you have to bear the weight of my sins and of Edward's folly," I murmured. "That you are the person burdened with putting everything right."

Richard sat for many moments. Finally, he rose and kissed me on the cheek.

"I thank you," he whispered softly. "You have given me the strength I need. It shall be done."

Chapter 31
Berkhamsted Castle, Hertfordshire
September 1483

Madam,

I beseech you most humbly for your daily blessing and prayers for matters have been accomplished which you know of. I make a solemn oath that I will found a chantry at York, where one hundred priests will say masses for my soul.

Written at York, the eighth day of September, in the first year of our reign, by the hand of your most humble son,

Ricardus Rex

I wobbled and sank into my seat, motioning Gerard to rise. He was now in his early forties, remaining at my side since the day I'd arrived at Berkhamsted some fourteen years before.

"How did it happen?"

Gerard hesitated.

"I must pray for my sins, of which there are many. But I cannot take responsibility for something if you keep me in the dark."

"Tyrell saw to it." Sir James Tyrell worked as a secretary in Richard's household.

"And?"

"Smothered," he said hoarsely.

My stomach churned. I sat up in my seat.

"They were smothered in their beds in the dead of night," continued Gerard.

"When?"

"The night of September third to fourth. Tyrell had to leave London at first light on the fourth to make it back to York on September the eighth for the investiture of Lord Richard's son, Edward. He left York on the night of August thirtieth to London to collect robes and wall-hangings for the investiture."

Richard's son and only child, seven-year-old Edward of Middleham, had been made *Prince of Wales* in a special ceremony held in York on September 8, 1483. It took about four days of fast riding to travel between London and York, a distance of some two hundred miles.

"Did they suffer?"

"I don't know." He avoided my eyes.

I rose. "Where are they buried?"

"Under the stairs in the White Tower. In a chest."

I rubbed my hands together to warm them. "Master Gerard, this has been most painful—"

"I'll not work for you no more," he growled.

"Gerard!"

"That was evil," he spat. "Pure evil."

"Gerard," I said, putting my hand on his arm, "You don't understand."

"I understand full well!" he exclaimed, glaring. "You murdered those two boys, innocent lambs they be. Why couldn't you let them live?"

"Because," said I, sinking wearily into my chair, "if they'd lived, we would have been killed."

"They wouldn't have killed you. They had the souls of angels."

"Maybe not, but their mother would have. She had to be crushed."

Gerard was silent for a moment, considering. "And would that have been so bad?" he asked eventually. "I mean, folk, they die all the time. What's so bad about being murdered? I mean, the way you done it, madam, you've put your immortal soul in harm's way. You will burn in hell *forever*. And I want no truck with that. I'm done. I'm going."

And he strode out, leaving me sitting in my chair, with the ghost-like forms of two boys filling my head. As I tried to reach for them, I felt myself turning to ice.

Chapter 32
September 1483 to August 1485

Richard didn't have an easy time of it as King of England. By late September 1483, rumors stirred abroad that the sons of the late king had met a violent end. In short order this rumor became the talk of the courts of Europe. Many switched allegiance to one Henry Tudor.

Henry Tudor, Earl of Richmond, was a totally unknown Lancastrian exile who would have remained obscure but for a chance meeting between his mother Lady Margaret Beaufort and Richard's cousin Henry of Buckingham, himself a male heir to the Plantagenet line and possibly angling for the crown. Shortly after my son's coronation, Lady Margaret—a formidable, highly intelligent woman—managed to persuade Buckingham to abandon Richard's cause and join her son's. I am not sure how she did it, but she probably played on Buckingham's fears. For the southerners were not happy that Richard's loyal northerners were taking all the royal offices, or that the so-called Little Princes in the Tower—Edward of Westminster and Richard of Shrewsbury—had disappeared.

Lady Margaret was a kinswoman of mine, by my mother. Like me, she descended from John of Gaunt and his third wife Catrine de Roet. It was ridiculous for Tudor to put forward a claim to the throne, for there were many descendants of the House of Lancaster abroad who had a much better claim that he. For instance, the King of Portugal and the Queen of Castile were descended from John of Gaunt's first and second wives.

It would be as ridiculous as if I'd claimed the throne of England on my own behalf.

In any case, it was unlawful, for the Beauforts had been debarred from succession by Richard II during the legitimization ceremony in the House of Lords that my mother attended in 1396. However, Lady Margaret Beaufort put ideas into her son's head, and thus Richard soon found his rightful claim to the throne challenged by this obscure upstart, aided and abetted by the treachery of his cousin Buckingham.

In early October 1483, Henry Tudor's fleet set sail from Brittany, intending to invade England, but a storm drove the ships back to port. In mid-October, Henry Tudor tried again, but on All Saints Day, Buckingham was arrested.

He was executed on All Souls Day.

On that day, Henry Tudor arrived in Plymouth, but on hearing of the collapse of the rebellion, sailed back to France and established a court in exile. His mother was detained, but only kept under house arrest in the care of her husband.

Richard returned in triumph to London. But on Christmas Day 1483, Henry Tudor made a solemn vow in Rennes cathedral that when he became King, he would marry the Serpent's eldest daughter, Lady Bessy. To counter this, in January 1484, Parliament met and passed the Act of Titulus Regius, formally confirming King Richard III's title to the Crown. It also provided legal aid to poor people for the first time in history.

In March 1484, Richard finally persuaded the Serpent to let her daughters leave sanctuary, for their presence there was a source of great embarrassment to him. She embarrassed him further by insisting that he swear an oath in public that he would protect them.

On April 9, 1484, one year after Edward's death, Prince Edward of Middleham died at the age of eight. The people attributed the loss of Richard's heir to divine punishment.

Worse was to follow. On March 16, 1485, Richard's wife Nanette died at the age of twenty-eight after a lingering illness that caused her to cough up blood. Rumors about his wife's death reached such a pitch that two weeks later, Richard was obliged to deny publicly that he'd planned to marry his niece, nineteen-year-old Lady Bessy—or indeed, that he'd had an unsavory liaison with her. I promised to see about finding a suitable bride, for Richard was young, nigh unto thirty-three years, the same age my father had been when he'd taken my mother as his second wife. The best way to put an end to such ugly gossip, as well as the Serpent's plots, was for him to marry abroad.

But reports from abroad were alarming, for Henry Tudor planned another invasion of England. Richard put aside thoughts of marriage, meticulously planning to fight for his throne. He chose Nottingham as his residence for the summer of 1485 for its central location. If Tudor landed in Wales, as seemed probable—for he was Welsh on his father's side—it would be easy for Richard to gather his forces to meet him.

On his way to Nottingham, Richard came to celebrate my birthday at Berkhamsted. For on May 3, the Feast of Saint Philip, I turned three-score and ten years, the biblical end of life. During his visit, he asked my opinion about the special ceremony he would hold before the coming battle commenced. Richard wanted to start afresh with his people, who continued to be wary of him after two years of rule.

"You must send for holy oil," I said. "Ask the priests to anoint you before battle. The anointing should take place in public, during a solemn Mass."

I paused to let Richard write down what I was saying.

"And you should also send for the coronation crown of Saint Edward."

"But, Mother, that's unheard of. The coronation crown is sacred. I could not take that with me into battle."

"The crown is *holy*," I replied. "It will give you additional authority and protection. You must wear it in procession at dawn on the day of battle."

Richard bent over his parchment again.

"The priests should go before you wearing their vestments and holding up their crosses. Then you should ride out in full armor, with Saint Edward's crown on your head. God will give you his blessing, and then you can overcome the tragedies of the past two years."

I paused, smiling at the magnificent image this created. Would this ceremony work? Would Richard truly be able to start anew with his people? Only if his people wanted it. So who would be against it?

I turned to Richard. "Be wary of my Lord Stanley."

Lord Thomas Stanley's motto was *Sans Changer*, or *Without Change*. And it is true he'd been loyal to Richard during Tudor's abortive plot to take the throne some two years before. But he was married to Tudor's mother, Lady Margaret, and his ability to avoid all the major battles of the recent war was second to none.

"If I may say so, my son," I said, chafing my hands because they had suddenly gone cold, "you have been far too lenient towards Stanley, especially towards his wife, Lady Margaret. She is the real threat, for she is Tudor's mother."

"But a woman cannot do much," began Richard when he saw my raised eyebrows.

"You know better than that!" I exclaimed. "A woman may do as much as any man, given the opportunity." I drew myself up. "Lady Margaret is dangerous. Believe me, Tudor would be nowhere without his mother. She is the brains behind this campaign. She has the means, she knows everyone, she is here. That manor of hers at Collyweston is a beehive of activity. Heaven knows what she's up to."

"She is under house arrest in the custody of Lord Stanley. She can do no harm."

"I wouldn't be so sanguine. Clever women have ways of getting around their menfolk. Believe me, I grew up in a household of clever and resourceful women."

Richard laughed.

I could not helping smiling, even though I regretted the somewhat colorful tales I'd told him of my girlhood. Was there no way of penetrating through that thick carapace of male vanity?

I drew myself up again. "Be wary. Your father made the mistake of underestimating a woman. When his commanders pleaded with him to stay inside Sandal Castle, he said he wasn't going to be so cowardly as to shut his gates to a scolding woman whose only weapons were her tongue and her nails. That mistake cost him his life."

"Do not worry, Mother. I am going to crush Tudor. Never believe otherwise!"

How I wanted to believe him. So I put my sighs away, and smiled as he knelt for my blessing.

My son Richard was a superb king, fair-minded and just. During his reign, he reformed the justice system by allowing the accused to have bail, protecting them from imprisonment before trial, and protecting their goods from seizure until they'd been convicted. Unfortunately, he made many enemies, for folk did not know him and treated him with great suspicion.

Many folk, not knowing my story, regarded the Little Princes in the Tower the rightful heirs to the throne. The disappearance of those two boys ruined Richard's credibility and clawed at him for the rest of his short reign.

On August 1, 1485, Henry Tudor sailed from Harfleur, Normandy. On August 7 he landed at Milford Haven, Wales. On August 22, 1485, he confronted King Richard.

King Richard had the upper hand, his forces ranged on top of a hill while Tudor's had to slog through the low-lying marshes. But Richard, a true gentle knight, plunged away from safety to take on his opponent, just as his father did at Sandal Castle in 1460.

And like his father, he was viciously cut down and murdered at the Battle of Redmore Plain, commonly known as Bosworth Field, by that upstart Tudor and his followers.

Tudor did not have a good claim to the throne, and knew it. He also knew there were plenty of others who had a better claim. The rightful King of England was Edward, Earl of Warwick, poor George's only son, ten years old. Next in succession was his sister Margaret, who had twelve years. Tudor immediately clapped Edward, Earl of Warwick in the Tower, where he still languishes after ten years. Then he married poor Margaret to a knight well below her. A Sir Richard Pole.

My son Richard had no surviving children. Richard's designated heir, John de la Pole, Earl of Lincoln, was cut down by Tudor at the Battle of Stoke in June 1487. Other contenders were my bastard son's five daughters: Bessy, Cecily, Anne, Catherine and Bridget. They were luckier than the others.

Tudor sought to heal old wounds by marrying the eldest daughter, Lady Bessy. If only he knew how little that helped his cause, for he would have been better off with George's daughter Margaret. But by that time, no one wanted to believe the tale of my affair of the heart. They assumed that Edward must have been legitimate, because my lord of York never said anything to make them think otherwise.

What a hard world we live in. I little thought how my one night of transgression would cause so much grief. The dynasty now on the throne—the House of Tudor—is not legitimate. But what can I do? England has suffered much from my folly. Tudor seems keen not to speak of old mistakes, he governs on the principle of "least said, soonest mended." He and Bessy, my grand-daughter, now have children of their own.

Richard's sudden death in battle made me rethink everything. Should I have glorified his father in the way I did? Perhaps if I hadn't, he wouldn't have been tempted to make that suicidal charge against Tudor. Should I have done more to come out of retirement to keep Richard's enemies at bay? He was so vulnerable, for people did not know him. He was forced to commit a terrible crime before he could establish himself on the throne. Should I, then, have discouraged Richard from being king at all, when it was obvious the folk of London did not see him that way, preferring the Serpent's sons instead? Richard and his family could have lived in exile abroad. But would we have made it into exile safely?

Perhaps the biggest mistake I made was in letting my feelings for the Serpent get carried away. She was so easy to hate.

The hatred I fostered left poor Richard with some very bad choices when his half-brother Edward suddenly died. This is why I pray and do penance every day. I pray for the souls of the dead, for my sons and daughters, for my mother and sisters, and yes, even for the Serpent, for that poor lady passed away some three years ago, in poverty, at Bermondsey Abbey. She was so poor that her remaining son Dorset had to pay out of his own pocket for her modest funeral. Shockingly so for a former queen.

Tudor took her lands from her, claiming he was short of land. He forced her to enter a religious order, for she had nowhere else to go. Her only wish was to be placed at Bermondsey, where she could see the Tower, the place where her sons had disappeared.

An eye for an eye, a tooth for a tooth, two sons for a son.

How sad it all is.

EPILOGUE

She contynueth in prayer until the first peale of evensonge;
then she drinketh wyne or ale at her pleasure...
In the tyme of supper she recyteth the lecture that was had at dynner to those that be in her presence.
After supper she disposeth herself to be famyliare with her gentlewomen, to the secac'on of honest myrthe;
and one howre before her goeing to bed, she taketh a cuppe of wyne, and after that, goeth to her pryvie closette, and taketh her leave of God for all nighte,
making ende of her prayers for that daye; and by eight of the clocke is in bedde.
I truste to our lordes mercy that this noble Princesse thus devideth the howers to his highe pleasure.

FROM ORDERS AND RULES OF THE PRINCESS CECILL
QUOTED BY JOHN WOLSTENHOLME COBB (1883)
HISTORY & ANTIQUITIES OF BERKHAMSTED

Berkhamsted Castle, Hertfordshire
Feast of Saint Joseph
March 19, 1495

It is the Feast of Saint Joseph in March 1495, and I will have eighty years in two months. My mind drifts back fifty years, to another Saint Joseph's Eve, when Richard and I waited by the banks of the Seine for Marguerite d'Anjou to take her place as our new queen. Nan was with us then, young, trusting, and happy.

I am full weary of this world, glad to be leaving it. But before I go, I have an important task I must perform. I have written to my daughter Margaret, Duchess of Burgundy, to request a new Book of Hours. Tudor's spies will intercept that document. Let them smile at the fancies of an old woman. Let them think I need another magnificent prayer book. Let them admit a party of nuns led by an abbess, so that my memoirs can be taken back to Burgundy before that so-called King of England can pounce and destroy the truth about who is the rightful heir to the throne.

❦

I shiver with fear. The fire had gone down in my room, so I rang my bell. A nun appeared I did not know. This was not unusual; the sisters often take in new women as candidates to the religious life. I indicated the nearly dead fire, and she fed the flames. But I was struck by how clumsy and slow her movements were, as if she were not used to lighting a fire.

"Is that all, madam?"

"Yes, I thank you. You may go now." I went back to my writing.

After several minutes, I raised my head. She was standing beside me, reading what I had just written:

> *This is for my great-grandchild Henry Pole, grandson to my darling son George, and the rightful heir to the throne of England. This is the story of why you and your future sons and heirs should be sitting on the throne of England, and not*

that upstart Tudor, who styles himself "Henry VII, King of England."

As soon as our eyes met, the nun made a perfunctory curtsey and disappeared, letting the door bang behind her.

Who was she?

I hid my memoirs in my fur wrap.

❦

Half an hour later, the door to my chamber banged open, letting in a burst of cold air. I jerked my head up and my eyes met those of the new nun.

"What are you doing here?" I demanded.

"I brought these for you, madam," she replied, putting a goblet of red wine, one of my magnificent gold cups, and a platter of cheese wafers on the table.

I eyed these refreshments warily while she poked at the fire.

After banging around with tongs and poker, she sat down, drew out a ball of yarn and some needles, and started to knit.

I glared at her. "I don't remember asking you to stay, or even inviting you in."

"But your ladyship requires my company."

"I do?"

"Of course you do," she said smoothly. "A lady of your position and years needs someone to sit with her."

"I manage very well by myself. And now I wish you to take that tray of food with you and go."

She continued to knit.

I glared at her.

She ignored me.

I rang my silver hand-bell.

She got up, rolled up her yarn and knitting needles into her bag, picked up the tray of food. As she passed my chair she put my silver bell on the tray, then paused in the doorway. "I don't think you'll need that," she remarked, before leaving.

I felt the leather cover of my memoirs and smiled.

I fell into a light slumber. A blast of cold air made me sit up with a start. The door opened to Sister Ghislaine, cautiously poking her head around the door. "My lady?"

I moved slowly, for I was chilled to the bone and my muscles were cramping.

"I am cold and famished," I said. "This fire needs to be attended to, and I haven't not had anything or seen anyone for hours."

Sister Ghislaine's eyes widened in shock. "My lady. How dreadful."

As she poked the fire, bringing it to life again, I fumbled with my fur wrap. Thank heavens, my book was still there. "Where is everyone?" I asked.

"Everyone is here. Nothing out of the ordinary has happened. We didn't disturb you because Sister Dangereuse—"

"Dangereuse." I interrupted. "You mean the new nun?"

"Yes, my lady."

"What a strange name," I murmured. "Did you know Queen Alainor of Aquitaine had a grandmother named Dangereuse?" I snapped back into the present. "And what did Sister Dangereuse tell you?"

"She told us you were busy with your writing and had expressly commanded no one to disturb you."

Half an hour passed. I'd slumbered again when Sister Ghislaine knocked on my door.

"My lady, I have a tray of food for you, a light repast, and another poultice for your aching wrist."

She wound a tansy poultice around my wrist to ease the aching from all the writing I have done this day, then poured some hot spiced wine into one of my gold cups. She arranged dishes of pigeon pastries, lentils, and wafers on a small table. She stoked up the fire, for the room had become cold again. Finally, she put the silver bell back on my table.

"I thank you," I said, smiling at her.

Sister Ghislaine and I had become dear friends over the years, ever since my arrival here in the midst of a sleet storm in March 1469, twenty-six years ago. Ghislaine was a child of twelve, left at the house of Ashridge when both her parents died. Now she had taken her vows and was known for her skill in illuminating manuscripts.

There was a knock at the door. It was Mother Avisa, the Mother Superior who managed our Benedictine cell. Now a plump woman in her fifties with square, capable hands, she sank into a deep curtsey, then sat in the chair I indicated.

"Where is the new nun?"

Mother Avisa sighed and looked at Sister Ghislaine.

"I have searched for her but can find her nowhere."

I picked up the leather book made to look like a prayer book and secreted it in my fur wrapper.

"Very wise, my lady Abbess," remarked Mother Avisa. She cleared her throat and coughed. "I do not know who Dangereuse is, but I can tell you that I accepted her because she came with very good references. As you know, since Sister Matilda's death, we have needed someone who is a skilled herbalist."

"Who recommended her?"

"Her letter of introduction was signed by Archbishop Morton himself."

I gazed into her face. Archbishop John Morton was the new Archbishop of Canterbury and extremely popular with Tudor the Usurper. His popularity was due to a diabolically clever idea of collecting fines, known as *Morton's Fork*. Under this scheme, you either paid the original fine whether it was fair or not, or if you did not pay, then you paid another fine for not paying the original fine. Needless to say, Tudor loved this idea, for he was the most grasping, the most avaricious, the most penny-pinching monarch ever to sit on the Throne of England.

"Archbishop Morton is Tudor's henchman." I said slowly. "That plot against Tudor in which Lambert Simnel impersonated my grandson, the Earl of Warwick, was supported by my daughter Margaret. And we know that

Tudor's policy is to destroy anyone who might have a legitimate claim to the throne."

"Whereas my lady of Burgundy's is to annoy Tudor as much as possible," murmured Ghislaine.

I smiled. "She now has at her court another promising young man, this time someone known as Perkin Warbeck. It is possible that he could be one of Edward's bastards, dating from that time he had to take refuge in Burgundy more than twenty years ago."

"My lady of Burgundy also says he's another of your grandsons, the Duke of York," said Ghislaine.

I was silent. If that were true, it would mean that the Serpent had smuggled her younger son out before Richard disturbed her sanctuary. Could she really have done that? She was cunning enough, and desperate. I put that thought away, for a headache threatened. "Perhaps he is," I murmured.

❦

"My lady, they've arrived." Someone was shaking me.

I sat up slowly in my chair and blinked to adjust my eyes to the light of the candle.

Ghislaine was bending over me. "I'm sorry to disturb you, my lady, but they thought it best to arrive under cover of night."

"Whom do you mean?" I asked, my thoughts blurry from sleep.

"The party of nuns from Burgundy, my lady."

I sat bolt upright. "What hour is it?"

"Nigh unto matins."

Avisa bustled into the room. "It's quite a large party," she announced, rising from her curtsey. "Twenty men-at-arms, ten archers, a priest, three nuns, and the abbess herself. I have found places for everyone. There is someone who would like to meet privately with you now."

❦

I looked up as a figure swept me a low bow.

"Olivier de Blay at your service."

I looked at the figure before me, but couldn't see his face, hidden by shadow. I motioned him forward.

He bowed again.

Something familiar echoed. It was almost as if I were seeing Edward again. But how could that be true, for Edward had been dead these twelve years? Had my daughter of Burgundy sent me her latest protégé? What was his name? Oh yes, Lambert something.

"What did you say your name was?"

"Olivier de Blay."

"You seem familiar."

"I'm told I look exactly like my grandfather. Though I never met him."

He was dressed in a tunic of wine-colored velvet embroidered in silver. His stockings were a russet color. Of course. He had Blaybourne's build, nut-colored hair, long expressive face and shapely legs. But whereas Blaybourne's eyes had been hazel, this young man's were grey. I looked at his hand and saw a blue glint.

"Let me see your ring."

He drew from his finger a sapphire ring set in silver.

I took my sapphire ring from my finger and put both rings together. My ring nestled into the cutout shape of his sapphire, just as I had once nestled into Blaybourne's arms. My vision blurred and I fumbled for my handkerchief.

The young man hovered nearby and handed me a glass of wine.

"After all these years, I have so many questions." I indicated a seat, and the young man sat in the carved chair opposite mine, stretching his long legs out towards the fire.

"My grandfather was humbly born. His father was a blacksmith."

"He told me that," I said, "but where?"

"In the village of Blay, near Bayeux in Normandy.

I frowned. "His name was not Blaybourne?"

"Being so humble, my grandfather did not have a last name. But when he arrived at the monastery in Caen, the monks asked him where he was from, and so called him Pierre de Blay."

I smiled. What would Tudor say if he knew his wife had such peasant blood? I cleared my throat. "When last I saw him, he was dressed as a nobleman, and he had an entourage of pages, knights, and men-at-arms. That day, he gave his name as Philippe de Savoy, Count of Geneva."

"There was a gentleman of that name," replied Olivier de Blay. "He was the youngest son of Duke Amadeus of Savoy."

"But wasn't it dangerous for your grandfather to impersonate a nobleman?"

"He chose minor members of the nobility, and was careful in his choices. After all, the Count of Geneva never came to Rouen."

"I've always wanted to know more about him. I had so little time."

"Did you know he was a spy?"

I stared at my guest, as everything slid into place. The fact that Blaybourne knew so many languages. The humble background, the courtly behavior, the education at an Italian university. Even his advanced degree.

"I had no idea," I said, gripping the arms of my chair as I stared into the fire. The flames flickered, giving me an image of Blaybourne saying farewell to me all over again.

"He must have been in some danger while he was visiting me, for he had no protector."

The grandson smiled. "My grandfather was extremely well educated, and valuable for that reason."

"Whom did he spy for?"

"The Medici bank of Florence."

Yes, he had used that name when giving me his last instructions.

"Banks need information about which way the wind is blowing before they lend money," continued the young man. "My grandfather was trying to find out whether the English were likely to win their war against the French, so that the Medici bank could determine if it would be wise to give the English king a loan."

"Is that why he came from Pontoise?"

"Yes. After getting information about the campaign against the French, he planned to go to the court at Rouen to gather more information before returning to Italy. He was detained by a fair lady."

My cheeks warmed.

"The lady was enchanting, so I've heard," observed the young man smiling. "My grandfather delayed until he could do so no more."

"Until he had to leave," said I, conjuring up the image of the moment when Richard had announced his return outside Rouen Castle.

There was silence for a moment.

"He wasn't a nobleman," I sighed.

"No, but he could assume the guise of a nobleman. He said it made it easier to conduct negotiations."

"I always wondered how he managed to do that."

"The monks taught him his manners," replied Olivier de Blay. "As you know, some of them come from aristocratic families."

I nodded, too weary to pursue the matter further. "What happened to your grandfather?"

"He gave up the roving life of a spy, returned to Florence and worked for the Medici bank in other ways. Several years later, he settled down, married a young lady whose father was a wealthy merchant and produced a son. My father Cecilio."

"Cecilio?" I clasped my hands and smiled. "He remembered me!"

"He couldn't forget you."

"He was not happy?"

"He was well enough."

I looked down. Even when I was nine years old, marrying Richard hadn't felt right. Granted, I reveled in my power and influence. But had it been good for my soul? I examined my hands, now knobbled with arthritis. What would I have done had I known what that choice would entail? Would I have had the courage to leave three children and cause a scandal for a husband who loved me, in exchange for a life of study and companionship with Blaybourne?

No. For the cost would have been too high. True, I would have been spared the drama and tragedy of a life encrusted with power. But could I have lived with myself?

I felt inside my fur wrap and brought out the leather-bound book, handing it to the young man.

"My life is in my memoirs," I said. "Take this book to my daughter Margaret for safekeeping. For Tudor would destroy if he knew of it."

The young man bowed.

"Tell me more about your grandfather. Is he alive?"

"No, my lady, I regret to say not. He died some thirty-five years ago."

"The very same year as my lord husband," I murmured.

I leaned back in my seat, feeling Lady Fortune completing her circle. If I shut my eyes, I could see their faces: Mama's, Cath's, Anne's, Audrey's and Jenet's. They were laughing at something I said.

We were sitting in Bulmer's Tower at Castle Raby, discussing Chaucer. The day was warm and fresh. Mama smiled at me and patted my hand.

NOTE

Cecylee, Duchess of York died on May 31, 1495 at the great age of eighty. She is buried in the Collegiate Church of Fotheringhay, opposite her husband, Richard, Duke of York.

This manuscript was taken to Margaret, Duchess of Burgundy, who placed it in safekeeping at the convent of Roosendael just before her death, in November 1503. Unfortunately, this convent was destroyed in 1576, during the religious upheavals of the sixteenth century. The manuscript has only recently been unearthed.

About the Author

Cynthia Sally Haggard was born and raised in Surrey, England. About thirty years ago she came to the United States and has lived there ever since in the Mid-Atlantic region. She has had four careers, violinist, cognitive scientist, medical writer and novelist. Yes, she is related to H. Rider Haggard, the author of SHE and KING SOLOMONS'S MINES. (He was a younger brother of her great-grandfather.) She got into novel writing by accident, when an instructor announced one day that each member of his class had to produce five pages of their next novel. She took a deep breath and began. She hasn't stopped since.

Connect with me online at my blog: http://spunstories.com/

Author's Note

Thwarted Queen is set in the hundred years that led up to the Reformation in England. During Cecylee's lifetime from 1415 to 1495, the church in England was ruled by the Pope in Rome, as it had been for nearly one thousand years. The Wars of the Roses were therefore not about religion, for everyone worshipped in the same way.

Thwarted Queen naturally divides into four books. *Book One: The Bride Price* is about Cecylee's girlhood. *Book Two: One Seed Sown* is about her love-affair with Blaybourne. *Book Three: The Gilded Cage* is about Richard of York's political career from 1445 to his death in 1460, and covers the opening of the Wars of the Roses. *Book Four: Two Murders Reaped* is about Cecylee's actions in old age, and how she may have had a hand in the murder of the two little princes in the Tower. I used different points of view to convey mood and setting. T*he Bride Price* is written in first-person present to capture the freshness of a young girl's voice. *One Seed Sown* is written in first-person past to make Cecylee seem older and more mature. *The Gilded Cage* had to be written in third-person to capture all of the different voices and the complexity of Richard's political life. *Two Murders Reaped* is written in first person past, to capture the voice of the old woman that Cecylee became.

In thinking about Cecylee and what kind of person she must have been to have lead the kind of life you have just read about, I decided I needed a heroine. I needed someone that Cecylee could emulate both as an impressionable young girl and as an older woman. I chose Queen Alainor of Aquitaine, known as Eleanor of Aquitaine to modern readers. She was a real person who lived between 1120 and 1204. Like Cecylee, she lived to a great age and was the mother of two Kings of England; Richard I *Coeur de Lion* (*the Lionheart*), who reigned from 1189 to 1199, and King John, who reigned from 1199 to 1216. She repeatedly broke the rules of what was considered seemly behavior for ladies. Her first act of independence came when she divorced her first husband – Louis VII of France – and married Henry Plantagenet, who became Henry II of England. Later on, after she inspired her sons to rebel against her husband, he locked her up for sixteen years. However, she outlived him, and was let out of prison by her son Richard I. She ruled England for King Richard during his many absences, and won a reputation for fair dealing and wise judgement at the many assizes she held throughout the country. I saw in her the perfect role model for the young and subversive Cecylee.

Why didn't I choose Joan of Arc to be Cecylee's heroine? Because she didn't make her appearance until 1429, and the story of Cecylee's girlhood in *Thwarted Queen* covers the years 1424-1425.

The most controversial part of Cecylee's early life is her betrothal in October 1424. Most historians think she married Richard at that point, and the young couple went to live at the court of King Henry VI. Though this is certainly possible, I made the ceremony a betrothal because I found it hard to believe that Cecylee didn't produce any children for fourteen years. Cecylee was fecund, her children were born in 1438, 1439, 1441, 1442, 1443, 1444, 1446, 1447, 1448,

1449, 1450, 1452 and 1455. Although she was only nine years old in 1424, she could have started producing children by 1430, when she was fourteen turning fifteen. I reasoned that she was not living with Richard until 1437 at the earliest, and that the reason she wasn't living with Richard was because she wasn't married to him.

In thinking about who might have stopped the marriage, I noticed that her father died in 1425 when she was ten years old, and that Richard's wardship passed into her mother's hands. The person most likely to have prevented this marriage was Cecylee's mother Countess Joan. The reason for doing so probably stemmed from the fact that Cecylee was the youngest daughter and all of Countess Joan's other daughters had already been married off and left the family. It is also possible that Countess Joan did not like Richard. I used a fictional episode toward the end of *Book One: The Bride Price* to motivate her dislike.

It seems that Countess Joan was interested in literature. She may have leant two books to King Henry V (her half-grand-nephew) when he went to fight the French at the Battle of Agincourt. And Hoccleve may have dedicated one of his books to her. It is true that Geoffrey Chaucer was Countess Joan's uncle-by-marriage and so she probably owned some of the original manuscripts, which have since disappeared. I do not know if Countess Joan held a reading circle, but it would have been typical of the time period for her to do so. I understand that Abbesses would ride from one great house to another with provocative manuscripts tucked away in their saddle-bags, using the reading circles as a forum for subversive activity, rather like the women writers of Afghanistan who carried on under the guise of sewing circles, as described in *The Sewing Circles of Herat.* (Anyone who has read the *Wife of Bath's Tale* knows how subversive it is.) Apart from the *Wife of Bath*, I have also included some lines from Chaucer's *Parliament of Fowls* and the opening of *The Owl and the Nightingale* – which was written anonymously in around 1272 – to give a flavor of the times and some idea of the kind of literature they were reading. Of course I could not quote Shakespeare, as he was not born until 1564.

The songs were also chosen to be representative of the period. Blaybourne's chanson *Plus Bele que Flor* (More Lovely Than A Flower), and Cecylee's songs *I Cannot Help It If I Rarely Sing* and *This Lovely Star Of The Sea* come from the Montpellier Codex of the 13th century. It is quite possible that people continued to sing these songs well into the 15th century, making changes as they went along.

You may wonder why I chose to believe the tale of Cecylee's affair with an archer on the Rouen garrison. After all, Anne Easter Smith, who has written her own novel about Cecylee, dismisses it out of hand. I believed it both because it had a ring of truth to it, and because it explains so many things. It explains, for example, why Cecylee helped to nullify Edward IV's will shortly after his death, and why Richard III repeatedly sought his mother's counsel and seemed to have had a much closer relationship with her than Edward IV ever did. It also explains Richard of York's actions, why he had a sumptuous christening ceremony for his second surviving son Rutland, but not for Edward. And why he chose to exile himself to Ireland with Rutland, but not Edward. During that moment of crisis in 1459 when everything seemed lost, it is interesting that Edward sat it out in Calais with his mother's relatives, rather than being by Richard of York's side.

Of course, Cecylee's lover Blaybourne presented his own set of problems. Scarcely anything is known about him, except that he was an archer on the Rouen garrison during the summer of 1441 when Cecylee's husband Richard was away campaigning against the French in Pontoise. I was forced to make up everything about his life and circumstances and I tried to draw a character who was plausible for the fifteenth century, making him someone who would have gotten his opportunities in life from his education in a monastery.

To give a cultural read on the risks that Cecylee was taking, I included two stories about jealous husbands and the ways in which they punished their wives. Black Fulk, more commonly known in Anjou as *Foulques Nerra*, was Count of Anjou from 987, when he was around fifteen years old, until his death in 1040. He had a violent temperament, so the story that he burned his first wife Helizabeth in the market square at Angers after discovering her in bed with a lover, may well be true.

When twenty-one-year-old Parisina (or Laura) Malatesta was discovered in bed with her twenty-year-old stepson Ugo d'Este, her husband (and his father) Niccolo III d'Este ordered their executions. They were beheaded on May 21, 1425, when Cecylee had just turned ten.

Beginning with *Book Three: The Gilded Cage*, the novel becomes much more factually-based as Cecylee emerges from the shadows. I followed the opinions of historians Alison Weir and Michael K. Jones in trying to reconstruct this period, especially Alison Weir's *The Wars of the Roses* and *The Princes in the Tower*, and Michael K. Jones' *Bosworth 1485: The Psychology of Battle.*

It is true that Cecylee's six-year-old daughter was married off in 1446. I do not know if this was Richard's way of punishing his wife for taking a lover, but Nan was forced to marry someone who was notorious for his cruelty. If you are one of those readers wondering why a six-year-old bride would be more useful than an older girl - given that she would not be able to bear children for several years - you have to remember that these girls were used as pawns in huge land transfers. The reason for marrying a young child now rather than later was because the family she was marrying into was impatient to acquire the wealth of the land that she brought as a dowry.

Obviously, there must have been a huge problem of child abuse, for these young girls were taken from their families, and sent off to live with their in-laws at the time of marriage. Legally, the husband became the child-bride's liege lord, which meant that he had total control over her. The child-bride was thrust upon the mercy of her husband and in-laws, in a situation that is not unlike the one that occurs in India today. This practice was not uncommon six hundred years ago. In *Thwarted Queen* there are at least two other examples; Cecylee's sister Alainor, who was forced into a marriage when she was five years old. When her 18-year-old bridegroom died, she was married to the Earl of Northumberland's heir when she was seven. The other example is Richard's sister Isabel who was married when she was about four years old to Sir Thomas Grey. That marriage was annulled for reasons that are not clear; but it is possible that Isabel was badly treated. By contrast, if the young girl was betrothed, she continued to be under the jurisdiction of her parents and lived with her family of origin until the marriage took place.

It is not known what happened to the little princes in the Tower (the sons and heirs of Edward IV). In trying to reconstruct what happened I have followed the ideas of Alison Weir in her *The Princes in the Tower*. However, not all historians agree that Richard III murdered his nephews, so I have given an alternative explanation at the end of the novel, in which I suggest that the younger brother, Richard, Duke of York, was smuggled out of the country and lived in Burgundy. If you are wondering why everyone is so certain that the elder brother, Edward V died in the Tower, it is because there are records showing that the poor young man was suffering from a severe ear infection in the summer of 1483. Without modern medicine, it is almost certain that his condition would have killed him within the year.

A couple of incidents in *Thwarted Queen* are based on the testimony of people alive at the time. Cecylee's tirade against Edward IV – in which she publicly announces he is illegitimate – is based on what Dominic Mancini, an Italian diplomat of the time, wrote. I have followed the historian Michael K. Jones' opinion that Cecylee was exiled to Berkhamsted Castle in March of 1469, and thus Cecylee's explosion occurred shortly beforehand. Echoes of this can be seen in Shakespeare's *Richard III*, except that in the play Cecylee's tirade is directed against Richard III. Shakespeare's play can be treated as propaganda on behalf of the Tudors. He did everything he could to blacken the character of

Richard III, and so one can almost treat the play as a mirror-image of what actually occurred.

The other incident is Edward's marriage to Lady Eleanor Butler. This is based upon the testimony of Robert Stillington, Bishop of Bath and Wells. It is not known when the marriage actually took place, but I have set it in April 1462, because it gave a plausible time-frame for Lady Eleanor to have had a child before Edward met Elisabeth Woodville, whom he married two years later in May 1464. As in the novel, these facts did not come to light until after Edward's death. People at the time had difficulty believing this story because it was so obviously in Richard of Gloucester's interests to claim that Edward's marriage to Elisabeth Woodville was bigamous. However, the story had the ring of plausibility for me, because Edward was a notorious womanizer who may have been attracted to older widows. (Both Elisabeth Woodville and Eleanor Talbot were Lancastrian widows. Elisabeth Woodville was five years older than Edward, and Eleanor Butler would have been about seven years older.)

As far as I know, there is no evidence that Cecylee ever referred to her daughter-in-law as *The Serpent*, though it is true that she was dismayed by Edward's marriage and the two ladies seemed not to have liked each other. I picked that particular nickname because I felt it conveyed volumes about how Cecylee felt about Edward's Queen. Élisabeth's name for Cecylee, *good mother*, is meant to sound disrespectful. It is meant to sound like *Goodwife*, which although it was a polite form of address for women, only applied to those of the lowest social classes. By calling Cecylee *good mother*, rather than *Madam*, Élisabeth conveyed her animosity towards her mother-in-law. The encounters between Cecylee and Queen Élisabeth are fictional, but are based on fact, such as the Queen's rapacious relatives wiping the aristocratic marriage market clean and Cecylee's resulting problems in trying to find suitable marriage partners for her children. Cecylee did style herself *Queen By Right* and she did move into the Queen's apartments, forcing her son Edward to build a separate wing for his new wife. The speech in which she tells Edward off about his marriage is based upon Sir Thomas More's account as reported by Michael K. Jones.

Writing about the past forces historical novelists to confront the fraught issue of dates of birth. It is often difficult to pin an age on a person, especially minor female characters, because dates of birth were not systematically recorded. The reader should therefore take the ages of most of the characters as approximations.

Documents from the time provided a fascinating glimpse of Cecylee's life in her later years. *Orders and Rules of the Princess Cecill* and *The Rules of the House* show a strong-minded yet kind woman running a tight ship at Berkhamsted Castle. I hope you enjoyed the quotations from these sources. In her will of 1495, Cecylee makes reference to two nearby convents:

> *"Also I geve to the house of Assherugge a chesibule and 2 tunicles of crymsyn damaske embrawdered with thre albes. Also I geve to the house of Saint Margaretes twoo auter clothes with a crucifix and a vestiment of grene vellet..."*

I haven't been able to trace a convent of Saint Margaret, but there was a convent at Ashridge, about four miles from Berkhamsted castle, and so I chose to place Cecylee's friends from her later years there. (In the fifteenth century, most people didn't think twice about walking four miles).

Such documents also give us clues to how things were pronounced. In Cecylee's will of 1495, for example, she refers to Fotheringhay as "Fodringhey", so I used that pronunciation in the scene where Richard talks about his favorite residence to Queen Marguerite d'Anjou.

Lastly, readers may wonder how I came to choose the name *Cecylee.* Not wanting to get caught up in the Cecily/ Cicely controversy, I thought it would be interesting to see how Cecylee herself spelt her name. Her will is in the public domain, and it seems that she signed it *Cecylee.* However, her handwriting is extremely difficult to read – it looks like the signature of someone who does not write much – so it is possible that she actually spelled her name *Cecylle*. In the fifteenth century spelling varied widely and great ladies like Cecylee usually dictated their letters and papers to scribes who came from different regions of the country and spelled things differently. According to the Richard III society, Cecylee in her lifetime was addressed as *Cecill, Cecille, Cecyll* but the most usual form of the name was *Cecylee*. And so I went with that version of the name, knowing that it would be easy for English-speaking readers to figure out how to pronounce it. (It is pronounced in the exact same way as the more modern spelling of the name, *Cecily*.) If I had been writing for French readers, I probably would have called her *Cecylle*, because that is closer to the French version of the name *Cécile*.

It was an honor as well as great fun to have Cecylee materialize from the fifteenth century and talk to me about her life. I hope you enjoyed reading this novel as much as I enjoyed writing it.

Cynthia Sally Haggard
Washington D. C., 2011.

Below is a selection of sources I used in researching *Thwarted Queen*, followed by a list of characters in the novel.

Books

Amt, Emilie (1992). *Women's Lives in Medieval Europe: A Sourcebook.*

Ankarloo, Bengt and Stuart Clark (2002). *Witchcraft and Magic in Europe. Volume 3: The Middle Ages.*

Anonymous 4. *Love's Illusion: Music from the Montpellier Codex, 13th century.*

Baldwin, David (2004). *Elizabeth Woodville: Mother of the Princes in the Tower.*

Cartidge, Neil (2001). *The Owl and the Nightingale: Text and Translation.* University of Exeter Press.

Chaucer, Geoffrey (1382/2004). *The Parliament of Birds.* Hesperus Press.

Chantilly, Musée Condé, Jean Longnon, Raymond Cazelles (1489/1989). *The Très Riches Heures of Jean, Duc de Berry.*

Cobb, John Wolstenholme (1883/2008). History & Antiquities of Berkhamsted.

Gies, Frances (1991). *Life in a Medieval Village*

Gies, Frances (1998). *A Medieval Family: The Pastons of Fifteenth-Century England.*

Hardy, Robert (1992). *Longbow: A Social and Military History.*

Houston, Mary G. (1996). *Medieval Costume in England and France: The 13th, 14th and 15th centuries.*

Jones, Michael K. (2003). *Bosworth 1485: The Psychology of a Battle* (Revealing History Series).

Landsberg, Sylvia (2003). *The Medieval Garden.*

Parlett, David (1991). *A History of Card Games.*

Ross, Charles (1998). *Edward IV* (The English Monarchs Series).

Smith, A. H. (1978). *Three Northumbrian Poems.* (Exeter Medieval Texts and Studies). Exeter University Press.

Weir, Alison (1995). *The Princes in the Tower.*

Weir, Alison (1996). *The Wars of the Roses.*

Weir, Alison (2009). *Mistress of the Monarchy: The Life of Katherine Swynford, Duchess of Lancaster.*

Whiteman, Robin and Rob Talbot Brother (1996). *Brother Cadfael's Herb Garden: An Illustrated Companion to Medieval Plants and Their Uses.*

Characters

(in order of appearance)

CECYLEE NEVILLE, DUCHESS OF YORK, QUEEN BY RIGHT, ABBESS OF THE BENEDICTINE ORDER OF ASHRIDGE (1415-1495).

MARGARET PLANTAGENET, DUCHESS OF BURGUNDY (1446-1503). Cecylee and Richard's youngest daughter. Married to Charles the Bold, Duke of Burgundy in July 1468. She had no surviving children, but became great friends with her stepdaughter, Mary the Rich, Duchess of Burgundy.

GEORGE PLANTAGENET (1449-1478), DUKE OF CLARENCE from 1461. Cecylee and Richard's second surviving son. Married to Isabel Neville, elder daughter and heiress of Richard Neville, 16th Earl of Warwick in July, 1469. Executed for treason in February 1478, by his half-brother King Edward IV.

RICHARD PLANTAGENET (1452-1485), DUKE OF GLOUCESTER from 1461, KING RICHARD III from 1483. Cecylee and Richard's youngest surviving son. In around 1472, he married Anne Neville, younger daughter and co-heiress of Richard Neville, 16th Earl of Warwick. He is the infamous monster of Shakespeare's play, an exaggerated re-telling of his reign written to please Henry Tudor's grand-daughter Elizabeth I.

HENRY BEAUFORT (1436-1464), 3RD DUKE OF SOMERSET from 1455, son of Edmund Beaufort, 2nd Duke of Somerset and Eleanor Beauchamp. He was the principal Lancastrian commander at the Lancastrian victories of the Battle of Wakefield (December 1460), and the Second Battle of St. Albans (February 1461). He was beheaded after the Battle of Hexham in May, 1464. He had no heirs.

HUMPHREY STAFFORD, 1ST DUKE OF BUCKINGHAM (1402-1460), best known as a military commander during the Hundred Years War and the Wars of the Roses, he was married to Cecylee's sister Anne. He was killed at the Battle of Northampton. in 1460.

HENRY PERCY, 3RD EARL OF NORTHUMBERLAND, (1421-1461), son of Henry Percy, 2nd Earl of Northumberland and Alainor de Neville, nephew to Cecylee. An important commander for the Lancastrian side during the Wars of the Roses, he was killed at the Battle of Towton, in March 1461.

RICHARD PLANTAGENET, 3RD DUKE OF YORK, (1411-1460). Cecylee's husband, he was murdered by the Lancastrians in the Battle of Wakefield, December 1460.

EDWARD, EARL OF MARCH (1442-1483), KING EDWARD IV OF ENGLAND from 1461. Cecylee's illegitimate son by her lover Blaybourne, he became heir to the House of York on the death of his half-brother Edmund, Earl of Rutland and his stepfather, Richard, Duke of York. Winning victories at Mortimer's Cross in February 1461 and Towton in March 1461, Edward was crowned King of England in June 1461.

EDMUND PLANTAGENET, EARL OF RUTLAND (1443-1460), Cecylee and Richard's first surviving son. Richard treated this child as his heir. He was murdered at the Battle of Wakefield in December 1460.

RICHARD NEVILLE, 5TH EARL OF SALISBURY (1400-1460), Cecylee's eldest brother, he was murdered at the Battle of Wakefield.

RICHARD NEVILLE, 16TH EARL OF WARWICK "WARWICK THE KINGMAKER", (1428-1471), son and heir of Richard Neville 5th Earl of Salisbury, and one of Cecylee's nephews. He was married to Anne Beauchamp, 16th Countess of Warwick in around 1449, becoming the 16th Earl in right of his wife. After turning against his cousin Edward IV, he was killed at the Battle of Barnet in April, 1471.

MARGUERITE D'ANJOU "BITCH OF ANJOU" (1429-1482), Queen of England from 1445 to 1461, when she fled England. In 1471, she was captured by the Yorkists, and in 1475, returned to France. She died in poverty in 1482.

ANNE NEVILLE, DUCHESS OF BUCKINGHAM (born circa 1411, died 1480), Cecylee's sister, she was married to Humphrey Stafford, 1st Duke of Buckingham, one of the commanders of the Lancastrian army. During 1459-1460, Cecylee was forced to live with her under house-arrest.

THOMAS BOURCHIER, ARCHBISHOP OF CANTERBURY (born circa 1404, died 1486) he was a younger brother to Henry, Viscount Bourchier, and therefore brother-in-law to Cecylee's husband Richard of York.

ÉDOUARD, PRINCE OF WALES (1453-1471). Son to Marguerite d'Anjou, and possibly Henry VI of England or Edmund Beaufort, 1st Duke of Somerset, he was killed at the Battle of Tewkesbury in May, 1471.

HENRY VI "HENRY OF LANCASTER"(1421-1471), reigned as KING HENRY VI from 1422 to 1461, when he fled England. In July, 1465, he was captured, and brought to live in the Tower of London. In May 1471, after the Battle of Tewkesbury, he was murdered.

HENRY OF BOLINGBROKE (1367-1413), KING HENRY IV OF ENGLAND from 1399, son of John of Gaunt, Duke of Lancaster and his first wife, the wealthy Lancaster heiress Blanche de Grosmont. He deposed King Richard II in 1399, becoming King Henry IV.

RICHARD OF BORDEAUX (born 1367, died circa 1400) KING RICHARD II OF ENGLAND from 1377. He was the son of Edward, the Black Prince, the eldest son and heir of Edward III. When his grandfather died in 1377, he became King of England at the age of 10. He was murdered in 1399 on the orders of his cousin Henry of Bolingbroke, probably by starvation.

JOHN DE MOWBRAY, 3RD DUKE OF NORFOLK (1415-1461). Son of John de Mowbray, 2nd Duke of Norfolk and Lady Catrine de Neville. One of Cecylee's nephews, he was the premier peer of the realm. He switched sides many times during the Wars of the Roses, but his intervention in the Battle of Towton was decisive in winning it for Edward IV. He officiated at Edward IV's coronation, and died in bed of natural causes.

EDWARD III, KING OF ENGLAND (1312-1377), reigned England from 1327 to 1377. Known for his consultative kingship, in which he kept his magnates happy by asking their advice on affairs of state, and by marrying his sons into the English aristocracy, he reigned peacefully for 50 years.

LIONEL OF ANTWERP, 1ST DUKE OF CLARENCE (1338-1368), second son of King Edward III, he married Elizabeth de Burgh, 4th Countess of Ulster. She died in 1363, leaving him with one daughter, Philippa, Countess of Ulster, who later married Roger Mortimer and became the maternal grandmother of Cecylee's husband Richard. After the death of his first wife, Lionel married Violante, daughter of Galeazzo Visconti. Some say he was poisoned by his father-in-law during the wedding festivities.

LADY ANNE DE MORTIMER (1390-1411), eldest child of Roger Mortimer, the wealthy Mortimer heiress was married to Richard, Earl of Cambridge and became the mother of Isabel Plantagenet and Richard, Duke of York. Would have been Cecylee's mother-in-law had she lived.

JOHN PLANTAGENET DUKE OF LANCASTER, "JOHN OF GAUNT" (1340-1399). The third son of King Edward III, he married (a) Blanche of Lancaster, (b) Constance of Castile (c) Catrine de Roet (Lady Katherine Swynford). By his first wife Blanche, he was the father of King Henry IV of England. By his second wife Constance, he was father to Queen Catherine of Castile. By his third wife Catrine, he was father to Joan de Beaufort and her three brothers. He was therefore Cecylee's grandfather.

JOHN DE VERE, 12TH EARL OF OXFORD (1408-1462), the son of Richard de Vere, 11th Earl of Oxford, he married the wealthy heiress Lady Elizabeth Howard,

"Bess" in ONE SEED. In later life, he became a Lancastrian supporter. He was convicted of high treason and beheaded by the Edward IV on Tower Hill in 1462.

HENRY BOURCHIER, 1ST VISCOUNT BOURCHIER (1406-1483), 1ST EARL OF ESSEX from 1461, he was the eldest son of William de Bourchier, 1st Count of Eu (a Norman title) and Anne of Gloucester, a granddaughter of Edward III. In 1426, he married Richard's sister Isabel. He appears to have died in bed of natural causes.

HENRY HOLLAND, 3RD DUKE OF EXETER (1430-1475), was married to Lady Anne Plantagenet, eldest daughter of Richard and Cecylee in 1447. During the Wars of the Roses, he was an enemy of the House of York despite his marriage to Richard and Cecylee's daughter Nan He was a commander at the great Lancastrian victories at Wakefield, where Richard, Duke of York was pulled off his horse and cut to pieces, where Cecylee's eldest brother Salisbury was murdered, and where Cecylee and Richard's 17-year-old son was murdered after the battle in cold blood. In 1475, he served on Edward IV's expedition to France. On the return voyage he fell overboard and drowned Some say he was thrown overboard at the command of Edward IV, his erstwhile brother-in-law.

PHILIPPA, COUNTESS OF ULSTER (1355-1382), was the daughter and only child of Lionel of Antwerp, 1st Duke of Clarence and Elizabeth de Burgh, 4th Countess of Ulster. Her father was the second son of King Edward III. Philippa was married to Edmund Mortimer, 3rd Earl of March in about 1368. During her lifetime, Philippa was the heiress-presumptive to her first cousin Richard II. After her death in 1382, her rights passed on to her son, Roger Mortimer, 4th Earl of March. When Richard II resigned his crown without issue on 29 September 1399, the rightful heir was her grandson, Edmund Mortimer, 5th Earl of March. However, the throne was usurped by

Richard and Philippa's first cousin, Henry of Bolingbroke, who became King Henry IV.

MARY OF GUELDERS (born circa 1434, died December 1463) QUEEN CONSORT OF SCOTLAND from 1449, QUEEN REGENT from 1460, she was the daughter of Arnold of Guelders and wife of James II of Scotland. She acted as regent for her son James III of Scotland until her death in 1463. When Marguerite d'Anjou fled north to Scotland in 1461, Mary at first helped her, later switching sides to support Edward IV.

ANNE BEAUCHAMP, (1426-1492), 16TH COUNTESS OF WARWICK from 1448, was the daughter of Richard de Beauchamp, 13th Earl of Warwick and his second wife Isabel le Despencer. She was married to Richard Neville, son of Richard Neville, 5th Earl of Salisbury. Following the death of her father, (the 13th earl), brother (the 14th earl) and niece (the 15th countess), Anne became the 16th Countess of Warwick. Anne and Richard had two daughters, Lady Isabel Neville "Bella" and Lady Anne Neville "Nanette". When her sons-in-law George, Duke of Clarence and Richard Duke of Gloucester fought over the rich Warwick-Salisbury inheritance, she was declared legally dead and "invited" to live with her younger son-in-law Richard Duke of Gloucester. It is not known what happened to Anne after Richard, Duke of Gloucester became King Richard III and her younger daughter Nanette became Queen of England. She died in obscurity in 1492.

ISABEL NEVILLE, DUCHESS OF CLARENCE, COUNTESS OF WARWICK and COUNTESS OF SALISBURY "BELLA" (1451-1476), elder daughter and heiress of Richard Neville, 16th Earl of Warwick and Anne Beauchamp. She married George, Duke of Clarence. in 1469, and died from the effects of childbirth in 1476.

ANNE NEVILLE, PRINCESS OF WALES and DUCHESS OF GLOUCESTER "NANETTE" (1456-1485), younger daughter and co-heiress of Richard Neville, 16th Earl of

Warwick and Anne Beauchamp. Married (a) Edouard, Prince of Wales and (b) Richard, Duke of Gloucester, later King Richard III. She died in March 1485, probably from tuberculosis, though there were rumors at the time that she'd been poisoned by Richard III, because he wanted to marry his niece Elizabeth of York "Lady Bessy" and sire more children.

PHILIP III DUKE OF BURGUNDY "THE GOOD" (1396-1467). Cecylee sent her younger sons George and Richard to the Burgundian court for safekeeping during the siege of London in February 1461.

THOMAS KEMPE, BISHOP OF LONDON from 1448 to 1489.

ANNE PLANTAGENET, "NAN", DUCHESS OF EXETER (1439-1476), eldest surviving child of Cecylee and Richard, she was married to Henry Holland, 3rd Duke of Exeter in 1447, when she was 7 years old. She divorced her husband in 1472 and in around 1474, married Thomas St. Leger. She died in 1476 after giving birth to their child Anne St. Leger.

ANNE HOLLAND (1455-1474), daughter of Henry Holland, 3rd Duke of Exeter and Anne Plantagenet, she was Cecylee's eldest grandchild. She was married to Thomas Grey, 1st Marquess of Dorset the elder son of Queen Élisabeth Woodville. She died in 1474, aged 19, from the effects of childbirth.

ALAINOR, DUCHESS OF AQUITAINE (1120-1204) mother of King Richard I *The Lionheart* and King John. Cecylee's heroine, she divorced her first husband to marry her second.

LOUIS XI"LOUIS THE SPIDER" (1423-1483) KING OF FRANCE from 1461. He was the son of Charles VII of France and Marie d'Anjou. Shrewd and often vicious, he spun webs of plot and conspiracy which earned him the nickname "THE SPIDER." When he died in August of 1483, few people mourned his passing.

LADY MARGUERITE DE BOURBON, (1438-1483), niece to Philip the Good, Duke of Burgundy, considered as a possible bride for Edward IV.

LADY JEANNE DE BOURBON, (1442-1493), younger sister of Marguerite de Bourbon, also considered as a possible bride for Edward IV.

ISABELLA OF CASTILE (1451-1504), daughter of John II of Castile, was also considered a possible bride for Edward IV. She married Ferdinand of Aragon in 1469, unified Spain, and became the mother of Catherine of Aragon, the first wife of Henry VIII. She was descended from John of Gaunt via his second marriage to Constanza of Castile.

BONA OF SAVOY (1449-1503), younger sister of Charlotte of Savoy, who was Louis XI's queen, was also considered as a possible bride for Edward IV. In 1468, she was married to Galeazzo Maria Sforza and became Duchess of Milan.

PHILIPPE DE SAVOY, COUNT OF GENEVA (1417-1444). Youngest son of Count Amadeus VIII of Savoy, who became the Antipope Felix V. Little is known about Philippe de Savoy, except that he never married.

AMADEUS VIII, COUNT OF SAVOY (1383-1451), ANTIPOPE FELIX V from November 1439 to April 1449. He was married to Mary of Burgundy, daughter of Philip II, Duke of Burgundy, and they had nine children.

QUEEN ÉLISABETH WOODVILLE "THE SERPENT" (born circa 1437, died 1492), eldest daughter of Sir Richard Woodville and Jacquetta de St Pol. Married (a) Sir John Grey of Groby (born circa 1432, died 1461), (b) King Edward IV (1442-1483). She was the mother of the *Little Princes in the Tower.*

JACQUETTA DE ST POL, DUCHESS OF BEDFORD "JACQUETTA OF LUXEMBOURG" (born circa 1416, died 1472). Married (a) John, Duke of Bedford (1389-1435) brother to King Henry V, (b) Sir Richard Woodville. She was the eldest daughter of Peter I, Count of St Pol and Margherita del Balzo of Andria. Jacquetta had no children with her first husband, but had nine daughters and five sons who survived to adulthood with Sir Richard Woodville, including Élisabeth Woodville, Queen of England. During her lifetime, she was widely perceived to be a sorceress, and was accused of practicing the Black Arts to secure Edward IV as a husband for her daughter.

PETER I, COUNT OF ST POL (1390-1433), was the son and heir of John of Luxembourg. Through his father, he was related to Henry III of England. Peter was also a distant cousin to John of Luxembourg (1296-1346), the father of Charles IV, Holy Roman Emperor. In 1405, Peter was married to Margaret de Baux (or Margherita del Balzo), daughter of Francesco del Balzo and his third wife Sueva Orsini. Peter and Margaret had nine children, including Jacquetta de St. Pol, the mother of Élisabeth Woodville, Queen of England.

SIR RICHARD WOODVILLE (1405-1469), EARL RIVERS from 1448, son of Richard Woodville, a squire from Maidstone, Kent, he was the father of Élisabeth Woodville, Queen of England. He was executed in 1469 by the Earl of Warwick, known as "Warwick the Kingmaker."

SIR JOHN GREY OF GROBY (born circa 1432, died 1461) was the son and heir of Elizabeth Ferrers, 6th Baroness Ferrers of Groby and Sir Edward Grey. He was married to Élisabeth Woodville circa 1452 and they had two children: Thomas Grey, who later became Marquess of Dorset, and Sir Richard Grey. Sir John was killed at the Second Battle of St. Albans in 1461.

MARGARET WOODVILLE, COUNTESS OF ARUNDEL (1454-1490), a sister to Élisabeth Woodville, Queen of England, she was married to Thomas Fitzalan, Baron Maltravers in October 1464, when he was fourteen years old and she was ten. Thomas later became the 17th Earl of Arundel.

CATHERINE WOODVILLE, DUCHESS OF BUCKINGHAM (1458-1497), a sister to Élisabeth

Woodville, Queen of England, she was married to (a) Henry Stafford, 2nd Duke of Buckingham, (b) Jasper Tudor, Earl of Pembroke and (c) Sir Richard Wingfield.

HENRY STAFFORD, 2ND DUKE OF BUCKINGHAM (1455-1483), son of Humphrey Stafford Earl Stafford, grandson of Humphrey Stafford, 1st Duke of Buckingham and Cecylee's sister Anne. He was married to the Queen's younger sister Catherine Woodville in April 1465, when he was around ten years old and she was seven. He was executed for treason by Cecylee's son Richard III on November 2, 1483, because he supported Henry Tudor's early bid for the throne of England.

MARTHA WOODVILLE, LADY BROMLEY (1450-1500), a younger sister to Élisabeth Woodville, Queen of England, she was married to Sir John Bromley in 1465, when she was about 15 years old.

JACQUETTA WOODVILLE "JACQUELINE", BARONESS STRANGE (1444-1509), a sister of Élisabeth Woodville, Queen of England, she was married to John Le Strange, 8th Baron Strange of Knockin.

THOMAS GREY, FIRST MARQUESS OF DORSET (born circa 1454, died 1501), elder son of Élisabeth Woodville, Queen of England, by her first husband Sir John Grey of Groby. Deputy Constable of the Tower of London, he was married to (a) Anne Holland, daughter of Cecylee's daughter Nan and (b) Cecily Bonville, a wealthy heiress. and a grand-daughter of Richard Neville 5th Earl of Salisbury. It is possible that this grand-daughter was named after Salisbury's famous sister Cecylee Neville.

MARY WOODVILLE, COUNTESS OF PEMBROKE (born circa 1456, died circa 1479) a sister of Élisabeth Woodville, Queen of England, she was married to William Herbert, Lord Dunster, 2nd Earl of Pembroke when he was fifteen years old, and she was ten. They had one child, a daughter named "Elizabeth" in honor of her famous aunt.

ELEANOR WOODVILLE, LADY GREY (1452-1512) a sister of Élisabeth Woodville, Queen of England, she was married to Sir Anthony Grey in 1467, when she was fifteen years old.

ANNE WOODVILLE, VISCOUNTESS BOURCHIER (born circa 1439, died 1489) a sister of Élisabeth Woodville, Queen of England, she was married to (a) William Bourchier, Viscount Bourchier, and (b) George Grey, 2nd Earl of Kent. Anne had three children with her first husband, and shortly after his death in 1480, she married George Grey and had one son, who became the 3rd Earl of Kent.

RICHARD I "COEUR DE LION" (1157-1199), KING OF ENGLAND from 1189. The third son of Henry II, King of England and Alainor of Aquitaine, he was known as "coeur de lion" or "the lionheart" because of his military exploits.

BERENGARIA OF NAVARRE (born circa 1170, died 1230), QUEEN OF ENGLAND from 1191, she was the eldest daughter of Sancho VI of Navarre, and wife of Richard Coeur de Lion. Richard's mother Alainor of Aquitaine supported this marriage, because an alliance with Navarre meant protection for the southern borders of Aquitaine.

MELUSINA (or MELUSINE) is a figure of European legends and folklore, a feminine spirit of fresh waters in sacred springs and rivers. The Counts of Anjou are supposedly descended from Melusina. Thus she would have been an ancestress of both Cecylee (via Henry II and Edward III) and Élisabeth Woodville (via Henry II and Alainor of Aquitaine's granddaughter Eleanor Plantagenet).

CATRINE DE NEVILLE, DUCHESS OF NORFOLK "CATH" (born circa 1397, died circa 1483). Cecylee's eldest sister, she was married four times to (a) John de Mowbray, 2nd Duke of Norfolk, (b) Sir Thomas Strangeways, (c) John, Viscount Beaumont, and (d) Sir John Woodville.

SIR JOHN WOODVILLE (1445-1469), brother to Élisabeth Woodville, Queen of England, he married Cecylee's sister

Cath in January 1465, when he was nineteen and she was sixty-seven. At the time, this was called the *Diabolical Marriage*. He was executed in 1469 by the Earl of Warwick, known as "Warwick the Kingmaker."

MARGARET DE BAUX or DEL BALZO (1394-1469) was the daughter of Francesco del Balzo and his third wife Sueva Orsini. The del Balzo (de Baux) family of the Kingdom of Naples had its origins in Provence dating back to the 11th Century. She was married to Peter of Luxembourg, Count de St. Pol in 1405, when she was around eleven years old and he was fifteen. They had nine children, including Jacquetta de St. Pol, the mother of Élisabeth Woodville, Queen of England.

SUEVA ORSINI (born 1360, died circa 1423). Sueva was an Orsini princess, and a descendant of Simon de Montfort and his wife Eleanor Plantagenet. She was Francesco del Balzo's third wife. They had at least three children, including Margaret de Baux, grandmother of Élisabeth Woodville, Queen of England.

SIMON DE MONTFORT, 6TH EARL OF LEICESTER (born circa 1208, died 1265) was an Anglo-Norman nobleman. He led the barons' rebellion against Henry III of England during the Second Baron's War of 1263-4, and subsequently became de facto ruler of England. During his rule, de Montfort called the first directly-elected parliament in medieval Europe. For this reason, de Montfort is regarded today as one of the progenitors of modern parliamentary democracy. De Montfort was married to Eleanor Plantagenet, one of Alainor of Aquitaine's granddaughters.

LADY ELEANOR PLANTAGENET, COUNTESS OF LEICESTER (1215-1275), youngest daughter of John the Bad, King of England and his second wife Isabelle d'Angoulême, was one of Alainor of Aquitaine's granddaughters. In 1224, when she was nine years old, Eleanor was married to 34-year-old William Marshal, who died after five years of marriage, leaving her a widow at the age of fourteen. On January 7, 1238, Eleanor secretly married Simon de Montfort, without the permission of her brother, Henry III of England. Eleanor and Simon had seven children. One of her descendants was Élisabeth Woodville, Queen of England

SIR EDWARD WOODVILLE "NED" (born circa 1455, died 1488) a younger brother to Élisabeth Woodville, Queen of England. Made Admiral of the Fleet by King Edward IV, he never married.

CHARLES OF CHAROLAIS, "CHARLES THE BOLD", (1433-1477) DUKE OF BURGUNDY .from 1467. The son of Philip the Good, Duke of Burgundy and Isabel of Portugal he married, as his third wife, Cecylee's daughter Margaret in 1468. They had no children. Charles was the father of Mary the Rich, Duchess of Burgundy.

ISABELLE DE BOURBON (1436-1465), daughter of Charles I, Duke of Bourbon, she was the second wife of Charles the Bold Duke of Burgundy. She was married to Charles in 1454, when she was about eighteen years old. They had one child, Mary the Rich, Duchess of Burgundy.

SIR ANTHONY WOODVILLE, (born circa 1440, died 1483) BARON SCALES, 2ND EARL RIVERS from 1469, eldest son and heir of Richard Woodville, 1st Earl Rivers and Jacquetta de St Pol. He was brother to Élisabeth Woodville, Queen of England. During his lifetime, Sir Anthony garnered a reputation for being a great jouster, a man of letters, and for piety. He was entrusted with the guardianship of Edward, Prince of Wales, later Edward V, the son and heir of Edward IV. In June, 1483, he was executed by Richard of Gloucester.

LORD HENRY PLANTAGENET (born 1441, died as a child), first son of Cecylee and Richard.

LORD WILLIAM PLANTAGENET (born 1447, died as a child), Cecylee and Richard's third son.

LORD JOHN PLANTAGENET (born 1448, died as a child), Cecylee' and Richard's fourth son.

LORD THOMAS PLANTAGENET (born 1450, died as a child), Cecylee and Richard's sixth son.

RALPH DE NEVILLE, 1st EARL OF WESTMORLAND (born circa 1363, died 1425). Cecylee's father. Married (a) Margaret de Stafford (died circa 1395), and (b) Joan de Beaufort. His marriage with Countess Joan took place in November 1396.

RICHARD WOODVILLE (born circa 1453, died 1491), 3RD EARL RIVERS from 1483, he was a younger brother of Élisabeth Woodville Queen of England and Anthony Woodville, 2nd Earl Rivers.

MARY OF BURGUNDY "MARY THE RICH", (1457-1482), DUCHESS OF BURGUNDY from January, 1477, she was the only child and heiress of Charles the Bold, Duke of Burgundy. She formed a close friendship with her stepmother Margaret of York, Cecylee's youngest daughter. Besieged by suitors, including Cecylee's son George, she married Maximilian of Austria in August, 1477.

AGNES WOODVILLE (born circa 1460, died 1506) a sister of Élisabeth Woodville, Queen of England, she was married to William Dormer.

CECILY OF YORK, VISOUNTESS WELLES (1469-1507), second surviving daughter of Edward IV and Élisabeth Woodville, she was Cecylee's namesake granddaughter. She was married to (a) Thomas Scrope, 6th Baron Scrope of Masham, (b) John Welles, 1st Viscount Welles, (c) Thomas Kyme, Kymbe, or Keme, otherwise called Sir John Keme or Kene, of the Isle of Wight.

EDWARD OF WESTMINSTER, PRINCE OF WALES (1470-1483), uncrowned King Edward V from April 9, 1483. He was the son and heir of Edward IV and Élisabeth Woodville. One of the *Little Princes in the Tower*, he disappeared in the Tower of London in July 1483, and was probably murdered shortly thereafter. He is unlikely to have survived to adulthood since he had a serious ear infection that would have killed him, even if he hadn't been murdered.

RICHARD OF SHREWSBURY (1473-1483) 1ST DUKE OF YORK from 1474, second son of Edward IV and

Élisabeth Woodville. In January 1478, when he was about four years old, he married the five-year-old Anne de Mowbray, 8th Countess of Norfolk, who had inherited the vast Mowbray estates in 1476. He was the younger of the *Little Princes in the Tower*. Like his elder brother, Edward V, Richard disappeared in July 1483, and was probably murdered shortly thereafter. Alternatively, he could have been smuggled on a boat to Burgundy, and returned to England in July, 1495, bearing the name *Perkin Warbeck*. Perkin Warbeck was executed by Henry VII in 1499.

SIR WILLIAM HASTINGS, (born circa 1430, died 1483). He was Edward IV'S boon companion and best friend and served him as Lord Chamberlain and Ambassador to France. He was executed without trial by Richard, Duke of Gloucester for conspiring with Élisabeth Woodville, the dowager queen of England.

ALICE CHAUCER, DUCHESS OF SUFFOLK (1404-1475), daughter of Thomas Chaucer and Matilda Burghersh, she was a granddaughter of Geoffrey Chaucer the poet.

ELIZABETH PLANTAGENET,, "BETH", DUCHESS OF SUFFOLK (born 1444-died circa 1504), second surviving daughter of Richard and Cecylee, she was married to John de la Pole, 2nd Duke of Suffolk in 1458, and bore him eleven children.

GEORGE NEVILLE (born circa 1432, died 1476) ARCHBISHOP OF YORK from 1465, CHANCELLOR OF ENGLAND from 1460, was a younger brother to Richard Neville, 16th Earl of Warwick, known as "Warwick the Kingmaker".

EDWARD OF MIDDLEHAM, PRINCE OF WALES (born circa 1476, died 1484), son and heir to Richard of Gloucester, (later Richard III), and Anne Neville.

MARGARET PLANTAGENET (1473-1541), COUNTESS OF SALISBURY from 1512, daughter of George, Duke of Clarence and Isabel Neville. In 1487, she was married to Sir Richard Pole, a cousin of Henry VII. Her descendants are the rightful heirs to the throne of England. She was executed by Henry VIII, the Tudor Bluebeard, for her continued adherence to the Catholic faith. But it probably didn't help her cause that she was so close to the throne.

EDWARD PLANTAGENET (1475-1499), 17TH EARL OF WARWICK from 1478, the son and heir of George Plantagenet, 1st Duke of Clarence and Isabel Neville, Countess of Warwick. Thrown in the Tower of London in 1485 by Henry Tudor, he was executed in 1499.

JOHN DE LA POLE, 2ND DUKE OF SUFFOLK (born 1442, died circa 1492), son of William de la Pole, 4th Earl of Suffolk and 1st Duke of Suffolk, married Elizabeth Plantagenet, Richard and Cecylee's second daughter, in 1458. A loyal servant of King Henry VII, he died in bed of natural causes.

ANNE ST. LEGER (1476-1526), daughter of Sir Thomas de St. Leger, and Anne Plantagenet, she was one of Cecylee's granddaughters. Due to the attainder against Anne Plantagenets's first husband, Henry Holland, 3rd Duke of Exeter, Anne's daughter with Thomas de St. Leger became the heiress to the Exeter estates.

THOMAS DE ST LEGER (died November 1483) was the second husband of Anne Plantagenet, Duchess of Exeter. He was executed by Richard III in November 1483, presumably for supporting Henry Tudor's abortive attempt to invade England.

RICHARD OF CLARENCE (1476-1477), youngest child of George, Duke of Clarence and Isabel Neville.

MAXIMILIAN OF AUSTRIA (1459-1519), THE HOLY ROMAN EMPEROR MAXIMILIAN I, from 1493. In August 1477, he married Mary of Burgundy. They had two children, Philip I of Castile and Margaret, Archduchess of Austria.

MARGARET OF SCOTLAND, (born circa 1455) daughter of James II of Scotland and Mary of Guelders, she was considered a possible bride for George, Duke of Clarence after the death of his first wife, Isabel Neville.

ANKARETTE TWYNHO, served Isabel Neville, Duchess of Clarence until her death in 1476. Then she served Queen Élisabeth Woodville. In 1477, George, Duke of Clarence took the King's justice into his own hands, and tried and executed Ankarette on the grounds she had poisoned his wife.

ROBERT STILLINGTON (1420-1491) BISHOP OF BATH & WELLS, from 1465, he served as CHANCELLOR OF ENGLAND twice under Edward IV. He married Edward IV to Lady Eleanor Talbot probably sometime in 1462.

BIRGITTA BIRGERSDOTTER "SAINT BRIDGET OF SWEDEN" (1303-1373); was a mystic and saint, and founder of the Bridgettine Order after the death of her husband. The most celebrated saint of Sweden, she was also the mother of a saint, Saint Catherine of Vadstena. She was Cecylee's favorite saint, and a book of her prayers was found in Cecylee's possession after her death.

LADY ELIZABETH BEAUCHAMP "LISETTE" (born circa 1421, died 1480), youngest daughter of Richard de Beauchamp, 13th Earl of Warwick and Elizabeth de Berkeley. She was married to Cecylee's brother George, Lord Latimer, and was a sister to Margaret Talbot and Eleanor Beaufort.

THOMAS ROTHERHAM (1423-1500). ARCHBISHOP OF YORK from 1480, he was one of the celebrants at the funeral mass of Edward IV.

JOHN MORTON, BISHOP OF ELY (1420-1500). ARCHBISHOP OF CANTERBURY from 1486, CHANCELLOR OF ENGLAND from 1487. Originator of "Morton's Fork" as a full-proof method of collecting fines.

SIR RICHARD GREY (born circa 1457, died 1483), younger son of Queen Élisabeth Woodville by her first husband Sir John Grey of Groby. He was executed by Richard of Gloucester, on his way to becoming King Richard III.

LADY ELEANOR TALBOT also known as LADY ELEANOR BUTLER (born circa 1435, died 1468), youngest daughter to John Talbot, 1st Earl of

Shrewsbury. She married (a) Sir Thomas Butler, (b) Edward IV. She was buried at the Carmelite Priory of Ludlow in June, 1468.

LADY MARGARET BEAUCHAMP, COUNTESS OF SHREWSBURY (1404-1468), eldest daughter of Richard de Beauchamp, 13th Earl of Warwick and his first wife Elizabeth de Berkeley. In 1425, she was married to John Talbot, 1st Earl of Shrewsbury. They had five children, including Lady Eleanor Talbot, the first wife of Edward IV. She was portrayed as Cecylee's dearest friend and confidante in ONE SEED.

EDWARD OF WIGMORE (born circa 1463, died circa 1468), son of Edward IV and Lady Eleanor Talbot.

RALPH SHAW (died 1484), also known as RALPH SHAA was a theologian and half-brother to Edmund Shaa, the Lord Mayor of London. He preached a sermon at St. Paul's Cross in the summer of 1483, on behalf of Richard of Gloucester.

JOHN DE LA POLE, EARL OF LINCOLN (born circa 1462, died 1487), eldest son and heir of John de la Pole, 2nd Duke of Suffolk, and Elizabeth Plantagenet, he was one of Cecylee's grandsons. On the death of Edward of Middleham in 1484, Richard III made him his heir. He was killed at the Battle of Stoke by Henry VII.

HENRY TUDOR, EARL OF RICHMOND, (1457-1509), HENRY VII from 1485, he was the son of Edmund Tudor, Earl of Richmond and Lady Margaret Beaufort. He won the Battle of Bosworth in 1485, in which Richard III was killed. He married Edward IV's heiress, Elizabeth of York in 1486, and founded the Tudor dynasty. He is the father of Henry VIII.

LADY MARGARET BEAUFORT (1443-1509) daughter of John Beaufort, 1st Duke of Somerset and Margaret Beauchamp of Bletsoe. She was married to: (a) John de la Pole, 2nd Duke of Suffolk in 1450, when she was seven years old; (the marriage was dissolved in 1453), (b) Edmund Tudor, Earl of Richmond in 1455, when she was twelve years old; (c) Sir Henry Stafford, younger son of Humphrey Stafford, 1st Duke of Buckingham and Anne Neville in 1462, when she was nineteen years old; (d) Thomas, Earl Stanley in 1472, when she was twenty-nine. Her only child was Henry Tudor, Earl of Richmond (born when she was thirteen years old). He became King Henry VII after the Battle of Bosworth. Lady Margaret was distantly related to Cecylee via her mother, Joan de Beaufort. She seems not to have had children after the birth of her son, and died only two months after his death, in June 1509.

CATRINE DE ROET (1350-1404), also known as Lady Katherine Swynford. Cecylee's grandmother, and Countess Joan's mother. She married (a) Sir Hugh Swynford, and (b) John of Gaunt, third son of King Edward III.

JOHN II (1455-1495), KING OF PORTUGAL from 1481, was the son of Alfonso V of Portugal, who was descended from Philippa of Lancaster, daughter of John of Gaunt.

ELIZABETH OF YORK "LADY BESSY", QUEEN OF ENGLAND (1466-1503), eldest daughter of King Edward IV and Élisabeth Woodville, and his heiress on the deaths of her brothers, *The Little Princes in the Tower.* She was rumored to have had an unsavory liaison with her uncle Richard III. She married Henry VII in 1486 and founded the Tudor dynasty. She was the mother of Henry VIII, and died on her birthday, February 11, due to the effects of childbirth.

SIR RICHARD POLE (born 1462, died circa 1505), a Welsh supporter of Henry VII, he was married to Lady Margaret Plantagenet, daughter of George, Duke of Clarence in 1487. His mother was half-sister to Lady Margaret Beaufort, the mother of Henry VII.

ANNE OF YORK, COUNTESS OF SURREY (1475-1511), third surviving daughter of Edward IV and Élisabeth Woodville. In 1494 or 1495, Anne was married to Thomas Howard, 2nd Earl of Surrey. They had no surviving children.

CATHERINE OF YORK, COUNTESS OF DEVON (1479-1527), fourth surviving daughter of Edward IV and Élisabeth Woodville. In 1495, Catherine was married to William Courtenay, the eldest son and heir-of Edward Courtenay, 1st Earl of Devon. They had three children.

BRIDGET OF YORK (1480-1517), fifth surviving daughter of Edward IV and Élisabeth Woodville. Princess Bridget is believed to have been entrusted to Dartford Priory, Dartford in 1487, when she was seven years old.

HENRY POLE (born circa 1492, died 1539), 1ST BARON MONTAGU from 1514, he was the son of Margaret, Countess of Salisbury and Sir Richard Pole, and thus the grandson of George, Duke of Clarence. He was married to his distant cousin Jane Neville, daughter of George Neville, 4th Baron Bergavenny. They had five children.

PERKIN WARBECK (born circa 1474, died 1499) may have been the son or foster-son of Jehan de Werbecque. His mother may have been Werbecque's wife Katherine de Faro. Alternatively, he may have been the illegitimate son of Edward IV and Katherine de Faro, fathered during Edward's enforced stay in Burgundy during 1470-1471. Or he may have been Richard, Duke of York (born 1473), younger son of Edward IV, who had been smuggled out of London by his mother Élisabeth Woodville. Perkin Warbeck was executed by Henry VII in 1499.

LAMBERT SIMNEL (born circa 1477, died circa 1525). Of humble origins in Oxford, his family background is obscure. Noting a striking similarity to Edward IV (who had many bastards), a local priest named Roger Simon or Richard Symonds spread a rumor that he was the Earl of Warwick, son and heir of George, Duke of Clarence. John de la Pole, one of Cecylee's grandsons and Richard III's designated heir joined the rebellion, and Lambert was crowned in Christ Church Cathedral, Dublin on May 24, 1487. After the collapse of the rebellion, Lambert was pardoned by Henry VII, who put him to work in the castle kitchens as a turn-spit. He later became a laborer and died of natural causes in 1525.

MEDICI FAMILY was a political dynasty, banking family and later royal house that first began to gather prominence under Cosimo de' Medici in the Republic of Florence during the late 14th century. The family originated in the Mugello region of the Tuscan countryside, and were, perhaps, doctors. Their bank was the largest in Europe during the 15th century, and allowed the Medici gain political power in Florence.

Fictional characters:

AUDREY, Countess Joan's maid.

AVISA, a nun at Ashridge Convent. She later became Mother Superior.

CECILIO DE BLAY, son of Pierre de Blay and father of Olivier de Blay.

DANGEREUSE, a nun at Ashridge Convent.

GERARD, one of the men who arrests Cecylee, he stayed to work for her at Berkhamsted.

GHISLAINE, maid to the Sisters of Ashridge Convent. She later became a nun there.

JENET, Cecylee's maid.

OLIVIER DE BLAY, grandson of PIERRE DE BLAY, Cecylee's lover.

PIERRE DE BLAY "BLAYBOURNE", Cecylee's lover.

QUESTIONS FOR DISCUSSION

1. Cecylee is a high-spirited girl at the beginning of *Thwarted Queen*. What does she want more than anything in life? Is it attainable for someone of her class and gender?

2. Cecylee is beaten and locked up by her father in his determination to force her to marry Richard Duke of York. What happens to Cecylee's three daughters Nan Duchess of Exeter, Beth Duchess of Suffolk, and Margaret Duchess of Burgundy? Were any of them treated as badly as Cecylee?

3. Were you surprised by Cecylee's affair with the archer Blaybourne? How did she persuade Richard to let her keep her illegitimate son? What did you think of Richard's decision to make Edward his heir?

4. Cecylee and her husband Richard seem close and appear to have an unusually happy marriage for the time period. Evaluate their marriage. What are its strengths and weaknesses? In your opinion, which partner benefited the most from this marriage?

5. Each of Cecylee's sons, Edward IV, George Duke of Clarence and Richard III has a very different personality. Which one did you like the best and why? Which son was Cecylee's favorite?

6. Were you surprised by Edward's marriage to beautiful commoner Elisabeth Woodville? Were you surprised by Cecylee's reaction to the marriage? Did you find her reaction understandable or unreasonable?

7. Both Richard of York and his youngest son Richard III die in a similar fashion. What drove both men to act in such a

way as to cause their own deaths? Do you think this reflects their personalities, or were other factors at play?

8. Cecylee outlives her husband by thirty-five years. Without her husband by her side and as the mother of the King of England, she has unparalleled freedom for a woman in 1400s England. Do you think she used that freedom well? Or do you think she needed Richard of York at her side to save her from herself?

9. During the lifetime of King Edward IV, Richard III behaves as a model brother, always loyal, always reliable. Yet after the death of King Edward, Richard's behavior suddenly changes. Why do you think Richard changes his behavior?

10. Richard III has a short and difficult reign as King of England. What would you say was the biggest mistake he made as King?

11. This novel traces out seventy-one years of one person's life. Cecylee begins the novel as a high-spirited nine-year-old. She ends as a sad, yet beloved, eighty-year-old. Which events in her life changed her the most?

5019033R00117

Printed in Great Britain
by Amazon.co.uk, Ltd.,
Marston Gate.